for

Love

of the

Marquess

The Noble Hearts, Book 2

CALLIE HUTTON

Author's website: http://calliehutton.com/
Cover design by Erin Dameron-Hill
Manufactured in the United States of America

First Edition May 2017

ISBN-10: 154640774X
ISBN-13: 978-1546407744

ABOUT THE BOOK

She will never trust her broken heart to him again.

Shortly after Lady Juliet trusted her heart to Graham, the Marquess of Hertford, he disappeared with no explanation. Eight months later he is back in London, eager to resume their relationship, but claims he cannot tell her where he's been.

Graham was fulfilling a duty to the duke who had once acted as his guardian. Sworn to secrecy, Graham is frustrated in his attempts to win back Juliet's trust and convince her he wants her for his wife. As he works hard to chip away at her frozen heart, a twist of fate might snatch happiness away from them forever.

PROLOGUE

London, England
July, 1818

The Marquess of Hertford looked up from the book he read as Stevenson, his butler, entered the library. "My lord, a note has just been delivered to our door." He held out a cream-colored piece of vellum with the seal of the Duke of Reading's crest on it.

Graham took the paper from the butler's hand. "Thank you. Is there someone waiting for an answer?"

"Yes, my lord."

Odd that His Grace would send a note around in the evening, and then expect an answer, since in most cases Graham would be out for the night. He would have been at the theater, in fact, but had no desire to attend social functions while Lady Juliet was busy with her sister's wedding.

He opened the note and read:

Hertford,
A situation has come up that requires your assistance. Please attend me tomorrow morning.
Reading

Graham smiled. It sounded so much like the duke. The man who had been his guardian from the time Graham's parents had died in a fire when he was a mere three and ten years. Graham had spent the time between then and leaving University as the duke's protégé, preparing to assume the duties that came with his title.

He scribbled his answer that he would arrive at ten the next morning and handed the note back to Stevenson. The man took the paper and left the room.

Graham checked the time on the long case clock in the corner. An hour before midnight. He stretched and considered visiting one of his clubs. What he wanted to do was climb through Lady Juliet's window and spend hours making love to her.

They'd been courting almost from the beginning of the Season, and just recently they'd taken the step that would have her father demanding marriage, except that was exactly what Graham had in mind. Juliet was precisely who he desired for his marchioness.

He'd wanted to speak with her father and sign the marriage contracts, but Juliet had asked him to wait until her sister's wedding was over. It seemed their father, in order to get his eldest married, had told Juliet and her two sisters that until Lady Elise was married, he would not accept offers for the other two girls' hands. Since Lady Elise and Lord St. George were a mere two weeks away from speaking their vows, Graham had thought it silly to wait, but abided by Juliet's request.

Despite the early hour, he had a small brandy, and then took himself off to bed, curious as to his morning visit with the Duke.

***

At precisely ten o'clock the next morning, Graham entered the duke's study. The man stood as Graham entered, a grave look on his face. "Thank you for coming, son. I appreciate it." He looked past Graham's shoulder at the butler who had shown him in. "Please send for coffee." He glanced at Graham, "Have you eaten?"

"Yes, Your Grace, but coffee would be welcomed."

The duke nodded and waved at the two chairs in front of the fireplace. Once they were both settled, Reading leaned forward, his forearms resting on his thighs. "I have a serious problem to deal with. Very serious."

Graham settled back, concerned at the duke's

obvious distress. "What can I help with?"

The man stood and ran his fingers through his hair. "I don't even know how to say this, since this is not a situation I had ever imagined." He took a deep breath and looked up at the ceiling. "Amy is with child."

To say Graham was taken aback was an understatement of great magnitude. Amy was the duke's only child, a girl two years older than Graham's seven and twenty. She was what was known as 'different.' A sweet girl, but very childish in her manner, and well protected by her father, who had kept her out of the public eye most of her life.

Beautiful, with curly blonde hair and wide blue eyes, Amy was lively and full of laughter, a joy to be around. The poor girl had struggled to learn to read and do her numbers. Anything else seemed to be beyond her. The duke had consulted several doctors over the years, and they all seemed to believe confinement to an institution was best. The duke threw the men out of the house one by one and continued to love and cherish his only child.

"How?" It was the only word Graham could get out. He and Amy had spent hours together when he lived with the duke on his estate, Euston Hall, in Suffolk. They'd run together, swam together, played games, climbed trees, and took their studies with the tutor until Graham was ready for University. He still remembered how she'd clung to him and cried when he'd left.

"The best I can deduce is she got involved with one of the staff at the Hall. She won't say—as you know she can be quite stubborn—and no one, of course, is stepping up, since they know the wrath that will descend upon the head of whoever is responsible for this. Rape is about all I can label it. She is certainly unable to offer consent for such activities."

Amy had made her come-out at eight and ten years, but after a few blunders, the duke had bundled her up and taken her back to Euston Hall. She'd lived there quite happily with her various activities of tending to the flower garden, sewing, and playing games with some of the staff. Until now, apparently.

"What is it you to would like me to do?" They might as well get to the crux of the matter.

Reading sat and studied him. "My sister resides in Paris. Now that the occupation has ended, I feel it is safe enough for travel. She is married to the Marquis of Agneaux, and has agreed to accept Amy into her home and see that the child born is placed into a foundling home before my daughter returns home."

Graham was still confused as to his role in this drama, but kept silent as the duke stared off into the distance. "Amy is unaware of our plans, and may cause some problems when the babe is born, but we all believe it is beyond question that the child must be given up and Amy returns to her life at the Hall. Although she will be carefully watched."

He remembered his former playmate as a sensitive, loving young girl, who, no doubt, had turned into the same type of woman. Since Amy was not fully aware of, or able to comprehend, the strictures of Society, he could see where she would balk at giving away a child born to her, regardless of the circumstances. 'Twas not an easy task his former mentor faced.

"What I ask of you, Hertford, is to accompany Amy and her maid to France. I would trust no one more than you. For several reasons, I am unable to leave London right now, and I cannot risk discovery of Amy's condition. It would ruin her."

Leave London to go to France? Just when he was about to offer for Lady Juliet? The duke could not have picked a worse time. The travel there, seeing Amy settled in, and then the return home, would take months to complete.

Then he thought of all the years he'd relied so heavily on this man. All the nights they said by the very fireplace and discussed Graham's future, and the assumption of his duties. The times the duke allowed the young, confused orphan to cry, without censure. He helped to shape Graham into the man he now was. How could he deny what the duke asked?

As it was, it must be breaking the duke's heart to see this happening to his daughter whom he loved tremendously. Despite the inconvenience, there was no other answer he could give the man.

"Of course I will accompany her to France, Your Grace. When will she be ready to leave?"

The duke let out with a huge breath that he must have been holding in. "Unfortunately, I would like you to leave today."

"Today?" He could never be ready for such an extensive trip on short notice like this.

"Yes." The duke stood and leaned his elbow on the fireplace mantle. "I have every reason to believe Amy will find a way to leave London and return home to" —he winced— "her lover. I cannot fully make her understand the repercussions of her actions. Since I have discovered what has been going on in Suffolk, she has become somewhat estranged from me. I am hoping getting her out of England quickly will avoid a complete disaster."

"I can take care of that, sir. I will have my valet pack as quickly as possible. I assume we will be using your carriage?'

"Yes. It is being readied as we speak." He looked at him with an awkward smile. "I knew I could count on you."

"I shall return about three o'clock. Will that suffice?"

"Yes. Amy and her maid, Mildred, will be ready to go. I don't think she will give you any trouble; she was always very fond of you. Over the years, she often referred to you as her 'brother.'"

That brought him a sense of guilt, since he had not visited with Amy in well over a year. He and the duke shook hands and Graham left.

The first thing he had to take care of was Lady Juliet. Even though she was not expecting him, he went directly to her townhome. The man at the door informed him that Lady Juliet was away and he had no idea when she was to return. When he inquired after Lord Pomeroy, he was told the man was also away from home.

Graham spent the next few hours attempting to find Juliet somewhere in the shops along Bond Street, and when that hadn't worked, he tried a few of the clubs to see if he could run down Lord Pomeroy.

Without success, he penned a quick note to Juliet, telling her he had to leave London unexpectedly and would write as soon as possible. Not feeling very good about the whole thing, nevertheless he appeared at the duke's house at the appointed time and helped Amy into the carriage that set off for Dover where they would catch a packet to Calais and continue to Paris.

CHAPTER ONE

Lady Juliet looked into her mirror at the sad eyes that stared back at her. It was her sister Elise's wedding day, and she should be happy for her. As much as she wanted to feel joy, all the happiness in her life had fled when Graham left her the night they'd made love in the very bed behind her.

He'd kissed her softly and said he would talk to Papa in the morning, but she'd asked him to wait until after Elise's wedding. Papa's edict that he would not accept offers for his younger daughters until Elise wed still stood. Even though Elise was close to marrying, Juliet wanted to make sure Papa had no reason to refuse Graham.

However, she had expected to see him at various events, and possibly receive an invitation for a ride. True, she'd been busy with her sister's wedding, but not hearing a word from him was frightening her. She hadn't seen him since the night they'd been together.

Two weeks. Two very long, very disturbing, weeks. She'd been tempted to send a note to his house, but held back. Something scared her more than his neglect. Had he decided after she'd given herself to him that she was no more than an easy woman, and one he would not want as his wife?

"Oh, Juliet, you look beautiful!" Marigold entered her room, dressed in a demure pale rose gown. Juliet's gown was also pale rose, but a bit more fashionable. Marigold had always seemed more than only one year younger than Juliet. "Thank you, sister, and you look lovely as well." She hugged her sister and stepped back. "I guess we should go fetch the bride."

Arms wrapped around each other's waists, they left the room.

"Elise, you are a stunning bride." Juliet sailed into her room with Marigold right behind her.

Elise studied Juliet in her mirror with a frown. "Juliet, are you unwell?"

"No, I am fine, why do you ask?" Lord, she never could hide anything from Elise. When Juliet had been only six years, their mother had died from consumption, leaving a devastated husband and three young daughters. Elise had stepped easily into the mother role, even though she'd only been ten years, herself.

"No reason." Elise continued to study her. Once her dear elder sister got a bug in her ear that something might be wrong with either of her sisters, she would not let it go. She considered it her duty to know everything about Juliet and Marigold and solve whatever problem they might be dealing with.

Even though, in a moment of weakness, Elise had confessed to her that she and Simon had been intimate, Juliet did not want to reveal the same thing to Elise. Her sister's situation had ended wonderfully. Right now, Juliet was not so sure hers would end the same.

Elise crossed the room and placed her hand on her forehead. "Are you sure, sweeting? You are not looking well."

Juliet snapped her head away. "I am fine. I just told you." Glancing at the look of surprise on her two sisters' faces, she re-arranged her features into something more pleasant. "Truly, I am fine. It is your wedding day, Elise. We must focus on you, and not on non-existent problems."

A glance in her own mirror earlier had revealed a pale face and an obvious loss of weight. Perhaps Elise had been so caught up in her own happiness she hadn't noticed Juliet, for which she was thankful. Now that her wedding day had arrived, her hovering sister would soon be off on her wedding trip and not be examining Juliet so closely.

Elise gave her one more glance and said, "Shall we go downstairs and see about this marriage business?"

Both girls grinned at her, and they left the room.

***

Two days later, Juliet descended the staircase and

entered the breakfast room. All the remaining wedding guests had departed earlier in different directions. She'd heard the last of the carriages rolling away from the house before she left her room. She was relieved to not have to continue acting the happy hostess, a role she'd never played before. Life would be very different with Elise married and living in St. George's townhouse

She was halfway through her breakfast, wondering what she would do with her time now that the frenzy of the wedding preparations was over, when the butler, Mason entered the breakfast room. He looked at her sheepishly, very unusual for their usually staid butler.

"Yes?"

"Please forgive me, my lady. A gentleman brought a note for you some time ago, but with all the wedding business, it got pushed to the back of the small table in the entrance hall and ended up on the floor. I just now noticed it."

"That is fine, Mason. I understand things have been a little hectic lately." She reached out and took the missive from him. The butler left the room, and with shaky hands Juliet opened the note.

J—

My deepest apologizes, but something has come up that makes it necessary for me to leave London. I will write as soon as possible.

G—

She frowned and read the note several times. However, no matter how many times she read it, the words did not change. Graham had left London, giving no indication how long he would be gone, or where he'd gone. Had he been called back to his estate for a problem that only he could handle?

Her initial relief at having received word from him did not last long. Was this his way of extraditing himself from what he now considered a sticky situation? Thankfully, her courses had started only a few days after their encounter, so that worry was no longer a threat.

Very well, she would take his word for it. He was called away, and would send news soon. She would carry on, and most likely a letter would arrive shortly, since Mason said the note had been delivered some time ago. Graham's estate was not so far that he could not write to her presently.

Feeling better, she decided to make morning calls. She would see if Marigold wanted to attend with her.

The days went by, and no word from Graham. Each time she questioned Mason on the arrival of the mail, she felt worse. In desperation, she'd broken with propriety, and sent a note to Graham's country home, Hertford Place. No response.

There was only one conclusion she could

draw. Once he'd learned she was not a woman who held her virtue for marriage, he'd abandoned her. He'd lost his respect for her and decided she was not the sort of woman he wished to marry and have as the mother to his children. Her heart ached and her stomach was constantly in knots.

The few events she'd attended had been torture. Too many young ladies of the *ton* had looked upon her with envy when she and Graham had been courting. Tall, handsome, charming, titled, and wealthy, he had been a sought-after potential husband by many debutantes and their marriage-minded mamas.

Now they viewed her with contempt or worse, pity. No one seemed to know to where Lord Hertford had disappeared, and the rumors began to fly. Of course, she was at the center of all the assumptions.

Juliet returned from the Bowers soiree with a raging headache. Keeping up the pretense of not caring that Graham was not at her side any longer, or unable to speak with authority as to where he was had taken its toll.

She stood in front of her mirror and hated the haunted look in her eyes. Her clothes hung on her frame, and her pallor spoke of illness. Stiffening her shoulders, she left her room and went downstairs in search of Papa, who was precisely where she thought he would be.

Entering his library, she observed him as he sat, staring into the cold fireplace. "Papa?"

He turned to her with a bright smile. "Ah, my precious daughter. How nice of you to visit me." Standing in a courtly manner, he held out a chair and motioned for her to take a seat.

"I was just thinking how quiet everything is here with your sister married and off on her wedding trip." He sighed and took a sip of his brandy.

"Yes, Papa, I miss her as well." She didn't feel this was the time to remind him that his edict that Elise needed to marry before he would accept suitors for his two younger daughters had something to do with Elise being on her wedding trip.

"Papa, I would like to ask a favor of you."

"Of course, my sweet, what is it?"

"I find I am tired of the Season. Now that Elise is happily settled, I would like to return to the country."

Papa studied her a bit too carefully for her liking.

"Is everything all right with you, my dear?"

"Yes. I just wish for some peace and quiet after all the madness of the wedding." Although that was true, she also felt a strong draw to retire to the place she'd love since she was a child. To lick her wounds.

"Sweeting, I think you have offered a wonderful solution for us all. Marigold has mentioned a desire to return to the country as well." He slapped his hands on his thighs and stood. "So be it. We will all return to the Manor as soon as we are packed."

Juliet released a sigh of relief, and gave her papa a fierce hug and kiss on the cheek, which had him studying her carefully. Before he could ask any further questions, she turned and left the room. Maybe at the Manor she would be able to put Lord Hertford out of her mind forever. Which seemed precisely what he had done to her

CHAPTER TWO

London, England
Eight months later

The Marquess of Hertford handed his invitation to the butler by the head of the stairs at the Crawford ball in celebration of the lord's youngest daughter's debut into Society. He scanned the crowd, as he'd done at every event he'd attended in the past week since his return to London society.

The first thing he'd done upon his return was call at Pomeroy House, but was informed Lady Juliet was unavailable. Three times. He accepted the information the first time, but after two more tries—both times leaving his card with a note scrawled on the back—he began to believe something was amiss.

Juliet might be upset at his quick departure months ago, but he had left her a note, and followed up with several letters to both her townhouse and country estate. None had been answered.

It might take some maneuvering on his part, but he would make sure they picked up where they'd left off eight months before. He was anxious to speak with her father and get the marriage contracts drawn up. If anything, being away from her for eight months had convinced him she was the wife he wanted.

Those months had been difficult in more ways than one. Amy had turned into a weeping, angry young woman, determined to escape his protection at any cost. The problem, of course, was her innocence and complete lack of awareness of how dangerous it would be for her to attempt a return to her family's estate.

She begged to go back to Reading Hall and marry the man who had fathered her baby. He doubted very much if whoever had taken advantage of her, had matrimony on his mind. His muscles tightened every time he thought about the scoundrel and what he would like to do to him if given the opportunity.

Due to those issues, when they arrived at Lady Agneaux's home in Paris, Graham had been irritated to learn Lord Agneaux was away from home and was not expected for weeks. Afraid if he left Amy in Lady Agneaux' care alone she would attempt to return to England, he was forced to remain there until Agneaux's return, which hadn't been for a good two months after they'd arrived.

Once back in England, he'd been forced to

travel directly to his estate to handle matters that had arisen in his absence. Consequently, he was only able to return to London a mere two weeks ago. And so far, he'd been unable to speak with Juliet.

He accepted a glass of champagne from a passing footman, and wandered the room, speaking with several people, always watching for Juliet.

"Oh, my lord, how lovely to see you returned to London." Lady Catherine smiled brightly at him. She had been one of the young ladies he'd flirted with last Season before he'd discovered his perfect match in Lady Juliet. After that, he'd had eyes for no one else.

"Good evening, Lady Catherine. I am happy to back among friends." He bent over her hand and bowed. "I assume you are well?"

"Yes, I am perfectly fine, my lord." She tapped him on the arm with her fan. "However, I don't see your name on my dance card." She dangled it in front of his face. He grinned and wrote his name next to a cotillion, still hoping to find Juliet in the crowd and have a waltz with her.

A half hour later, when Graham had decided it might be best to leave and try the other two events being held this evening, his head whipped around at the butler's announcement of The Right Honorable the Earl of Pomeroy, with Lady Juliet, and Lady Marigold.

His eyes ate her up. She was thinner than

he'd remembered, her face not quite as open and approachable. Juliet had always enjoyed *ton* events, and took great pleasure in dancing, flirting, and teasing. This woman's demeanor was almost—for lack of a better word—brittle. He watched her and her family descended the stairs.

Immediately, she was surrounded by men greeting her and writing their names on her dance card. He took a calming breath, and made his way across the room, cutting short any conversations various guests attempted with him. His focus was solely on the beautiful woman dressed in deep green silk, her lips smiling, her eyes cold.

It took him a few minutes to make his way through the men still encircling her. Her laughter, once deep and musical, now sounded shrill. Whatever had happened to Juliet?

She was speaking to Lord Benson on her right when he approached her from the left. Once again, her familiar scent of lilacs wafted over him, bringing back many pleasant memories. "My lady." His voice was soft, but she must have recognized it because she immediately stiffened, and after a moment, turned in his direction.

Any suspicions he'd had of her manner being vastly different from what he'd remembered was immediately confirmed as she gave him a steely look. With slightly raised brows, her hostile eyes viewed him and she said, "Lord Hertford, is it not?"

His mouth dried up and he merely nodded,

unable to reconcile his soft, warm, loving Lady Juliet with this woman. "Yes, my lady." He bowed over her hand. "I would request the honor of a dance."

***

Shocked beyond measure, and without hesitation, Juliet responded, "I am sorry, my lord. My dance card is full." Then she turned her back on the cad and walked away, for all intents and purposes giving him the cut direct.

How dare he walk up to her like he had never abandoned her and then hadn't contacted her for months? She'd received a letter from him that had gone to her townhouse, and then forwarded to the Manor. That letter had merely been a second notification that he'd been called away and would call upon her once he returned. No explanation, no indication what or where had demanded his immediate presence.

One of the grooms at her estate had a cousin who worked at Graham's country estate. Although she'd hated to do it, months after she'd returned from London, she had the groom inquire about the lord of the manor at Hertford Place, who had confirmed Graham had not been to his estate for months.

The answer to her question had been easy. Graham had seduced her, then left for parts unknown, not at all concerned if there had been consequences. Most likely her previous assumption that he'd decided if she was willing to give herself to him without benefit of marriage, she was an easy woman and not worthy of the title of Marchioness of Hertford.

Since she'd accepted that, why did she now feel as though she were shattering into a million pieces right here in the middle of the Crawford's ball? It was difficult to get a full breath—curse her stays—and all she could do was stumble through the throng, ignoring those who attempted to speak with her. She needed to reach the ladies' retiring room, despite the dances that had been promised.

Holding her head high and pretending all was well, she finally reached the door and entered the room set aside to restore the ladies. Even though she was away from the crowd, she was unable to fall apart since the few ladies already in the room would love more than anything to have something new about which to gossip.

She sat at one of the dressing tables and with shaky hands fussed with her hair. The face that stared back at her was almost a stranger. She viewed a woman who'd had her heart ripped out and stomped upon, and who would never allow anyone the opportunity to do so again.

Certainly, she would marry one day. It was inevitable in her world, and her sister Marigold would not be able to marry unless Juliet did first, according to Papa's edict. Drat that edit. She would be content with a spinster's life, loving her sister Elise's children, and avoiding men for the rest of her life.

After about fifteen minutes, while she calmed herself and allowed the maid to lead her to a swooning couch to rest with a cool lavender cloth on her head, she felt more herself and returned to the ballroom. Thankfully, Graham was not outside the room waiting for her. With any luck, he would have left the ball, never to trouble her again.

Lord Ambrose approached her as she entered the ballroom. He bowed. "My lady, I believe this is our dance."

He led her to the dance floor for a lively country reel which was just the thing to work off the rest of her anxiety. Ambrose was a pleasant man, and had offered a bit of attention to her since the Season had started. He was a viscount, wealthy, and charming. But she'd felt nothing for him when he'd stolen a kiss in a dark garden.

She had to remind herself that was precisely what she wanted. If she were forced to marry, it would be to a man who she felt affection and respect for, but would never fall in love with. Her heart had been broken, and she intended to keep it that way.

Over the course of the next hour or so, she spotted Graham several times, always staring at her. She pretended to ignore him, but it was almost as if his eyes bored a hole in her, not allowing her to shake the mixed feelings his scrutiny caused. He led a few women to the dance floor, seemed to only give them cursory attention, his eyes still seeking her out. It had become almost a game. She sought him out, pretending to ignore him, while he searched for her, making his notice obvious to all.

By the time the final waltz was announced, Juliet was exhausted. More from the strain of the evening, than from activity, despite busy with partners for all the dances. She looked at her dance card. Mr. Billingsley had requested the last waltz. She would look forward to finding Papa in the card room after the dance and ask him to send for the carriage.

Mr. Billingsley walked up to her, with Graham right behind him. Billingsley bowed. "My lady, I believe this is my dance."

Juliet barely heard him, distracted as she was by Graham's appearance. He placed his hand on Mr. Billingsley's shoulder. "I would consider it a great favor if you would allow me to steal your partner for this dance."

Billingsley looked from her to Graham. Whatever he'd seen in Graham's eyes was apparently only something men discerned, because he bowed in Juliet's direction. "If you will excuse me, my lady, I will relinquish you to Lord Hertford."

Stunned by the turn of events, Juliet sputtered. "But, my lord, this is your dance."

Graham stepped in front of Billingsley, and took her hand, raising it to his lips to offer a kiss.

"My lady?"

Oh, she should kick him in the shin, right here in front of everyone. However, Graham knew she would never create a public scene, practically giving him the cut direct before most likely as far as she would go.

She dipped her head in acquiescence. "My lord."

***

Graham breathed a sigh of relief. For a moment, he thought Juliet would ignore her upbringing and refuse to accept his hand. He entwined their fingers as he led her to the dance floor. Pulling her into his arms almost brought him to his knees. The familiar scent of lilacs, her soft warm skin where he placed his hand on her lower back, and the rightness of holding her brought back memories that had him aching.

"I would like to speak with you in private sometime soon.""

"Oh, dear, my lord. I believe my calendar is quite full for the rest of the Season."

He drew in a deep breath. "What game are you playing, Juliet?"

Her face grew red. "Excuse me my lord, but I don't believe I gave you leave to call me by my first name."

Knowing he was probably making things worse, he couldn't help it. He leaned into her and whispered into her ear. "I remember calling you by your first name while I pleasured you."

Her quickly indrawn breath had him bracing for a slap in the face, which he surely deserved. Instead, she tugged to free herself, but he refused to let her go. "No. I apologize, that was completely uncalled for. Please forgive me."

The tears in her eyes as she regarded him, with her chin lifted, made him feel many times worse. She shook her head. "I do not wish to make a scene, but I really do not want to finish this dance. Please release me."

"I will release you if you agree to accompany me to the patio. Only for a short time." When she tightened her lips, and gave her head a quick shake, he added, "Please, Juliet. At one time, we meant quite a bit to each other. I think I deserve to speak with you about what happened."

"You deserve nothing from me." Her voice shook and she blinked rapidly to remove the tears from her eyes.

He hadn't realized they had stopped dancing until another couple knocked into them. "Excuse us," he said. He pulled Juliet closer. "Please. We are making a scene. Come with me to the patio. I promise we will stay within view of the other guests."

Before she could refuse, or walk away, he took her hand and tucked it under his arm. They stepped around the dancers and reached the French doors opening to the patio. A few couples were taking the night air, so he led her down the steps to the garden below.

She pulled back. "You said in sight of the other guests."

Graham stopped right after the steps ended. "There is a bench over there," he pointed to a stone bench under a large oak tree. "May we sit?"

Juliet did not answer, but moved with him when he walked in that direction. "It is a bit chilly out here, my lord. Perhaps we should return to the ballroom."

"No. I intend to have my say. Here." He shrugged out of his jacket and draped it over her shoulders as she sat. Graham leaned his foot on the bench alongside her, studying her face. Yes, he had been correct. Something was wrong with Juliet. A great deal of the sparkle had gone out of her eyes.

"Am I wrong in believing that you are distressed at my disappearance?"

Juliet gave a very fake, very shrill laugh. "Were you gone, my lord? My goodness, I never noticed." She turned her head to look at the darkened garden.

"Juliet. Look at me."

She stubbornly ignored him. He reached out and cupped her chin, turning her head toward him. "Yes, I was gone from London for a few months. Then I returned to my estate where I had matters which needed my attention. I have just now returned to London the last couple of weeks."

She shrugged as if his explanation was of no

importance. He sighed and sat alongside her. "Juliet, please, talk to me."

"I have nothing to say to you, my lord." She stood and shook out her skirts. "It was pleasant seeing you once again. I hope your time in London is enjoyable. Should we meet again at an affair"—she blushed and glanced sideways at her words, which made him smile—"please do not request a dance because I am afraid I will embarrass you by refusing."

She turned to go, but he grabbed her hand to stop her, and stood. He placed his hands on her shoulders, and looked her square in the eyes. "Hear me, Juliet. I am not back in London to play games. I once told you I would speak to your father about us, which is something I fully intend to do. As far as I am concerned, nothing has changed. I still want you for my wife."

He swore she grew three inches as she stiffened and stared right back at him. "I am sorry to disappoint you, my lord, but seeing as how I will not dance with you, surely you understand I will never marry you."

He leaned in. "Yes. You will."

She did the same, until their lips were inches apart. "No. I won't."

Instead of continuing the argument, he moved the few inches and covered her lips with his. Before she could react, he wrapped his arms around her, crushing her to his body, plundering her mouth. Warm, sweet, moist. When she opened her lips, most likely to protest, his tongue swept in, tasting tea, champagne, and Juliet. Just as he'd remembered.

Her slight moan assured him she had not forgotten, either, and he still had the ability to stir her passion. His fingers gripped her head, turning it to take the kiss deeper. Just as he was settling in for a lengthy exploration of her mouth, she shoved him away, and wiped her mouth with the back of her hand.

Breathing heavily, she backed up. "Despite your low opinion of me, I will not be used again, my lord." She shrugged out of his jacket, which landed on the ground, and turned to hurry up the steps. Despite the public arena they were in, he called after her. "I will win you back, Lady Juliet. Have no doubt."

She never turned, but continued through the French doors, her form swallowed up in the crowd.

CHAPTER THREE

The next morning, Juliet's eyes fluttered open, and for the first time in months she did not awaken with a heavy crush on her chest. Odd, how she'd grown so used to that feeling. Now instead of the depression she'd fought, she welcomed the anger at last night's encounter with Graham.

So, he promised to win her back? Ha. He had no idea how determined she was to cut him out of her life. No doubt he planned to sweet talk her into his bed and then abandon her again. She no longer trusted him, nor wanted to trust him. Even though he claimed to be away, and then spent time on his estate, he never said where he'd been. The absence of that information was telling.

She threw the covers off, anxious to start her day for once. The excitement of matching wits with Graham and coming out ahead of the game brought new life to her existence. She would lead him on a merry chase, and then when she was finished, she would crush him under her feet, brush her hands together, and walk off and leave him.

Just as he'd done to her.

"Oh, Juliet. Look at the beautiful flowers you've received." Marigold greeted her as she entered the breakfast room. Several large bouquets occupied a place on the dining table, the sideboard, and two small tables near the window.

"Oh, how lovely." She went from one arrangement to the next, smiling at the cards. Mr. Billingsley, Lord Foster, Mr. Applegate, Sir Langley, Lord Browning, and Mr. Davidson. All the men she'd dance with the prior evening. She tried very hard to tell herself it was no matter that there wasn't one from Lord Graham Hertford. Had he given up so easily?

She filled her plate with bacon, eggs, an orange and a warm roll, and took her place next to Papa, and across from Marigold.

"I thought I would make some morning calls." Juliet looked over at her sister. "Would you care to join me?"

Marigold shook her head. "No. I never know what to say to people."

Although Marigold had always expressed the desire to one day marry and have her own family, Juliet often worried that the girl would never attract any suitors with her shyness. "It might help you feel more comfortable around others if you force yourself to make visits."

Papa looked at Juliet over the top of his

newspaper. "Leave the girl alone, sweeting. Marigold will do all the necessary things to impress the *ton* next year, when it is her turn."

Marigold smiled warmly at their father. "Thank you, Papa."

Juliet shrugged and continued with her breakfast. "My lady, this has arrived for you." Mason entered the room, and presented Juliet with one perfect red rose. I had just started to open, so the fragrance was wonderful.

"Oh, how beautiful." She turned to the butler. "Is there a card?"

"No, milady, just the rose was delivered by a lad. Took off before I could question him."

"Thank you." She set it aside, almost certain it had come from Graham. The man didn't play fair. Everyone else sent a bouquet. His offering was notable with its difference.

"I wonder who sent you only one rose." Marigold studied the flower. "How odd."

Papa snapped his newspaper and folded it, setting it next to plate. "Whoever sent it wanted to stand out."

Marigold nodded. "Yes. I think you're right Papa."

Papa stared at Juliet. "Any ideas?"

She shrugged. "No. None at all." Her reddened face gave her away since Papa gave a shout of laughter.

"My darling daughter, methinks you know precisely who sent it, and it does not make you happy that he did." He stood and kissed both girls on their heads. "What event are we attending this evening?"

"Marigold and I had hoped to attend the theater. Would you care to join us?"

"Of course. As your chaperone, I must see to my duty. Will any of your many gentlemen be joining us?"

"I mentioned it to a few last evening. Perhaps one or two will stop by." She truly enjoyed the theater, and unlike most of the attendees, preferred to watch the play and not to merely see and be seen. It was not always possible, but hopefully any of the gentlemen who might show up tonight would be interested in enjoying the play, also.

"Very well. I will be ready to escort my beautiful daughters to the theater. I will not be home for dinner, but will see you when 'tis time to leave."

One did not question one's father where he was spending his time, but Juliet had noticed he seemed to be away from home more the last few weeks than usual. Although to her he was merely Papa, she'd seen the way some of the women of the ton followed him with their eyes. He was not ancient, only about six and forty years. Handsome, and he still maintained a youthful form.

She picked up the rose and sniffed it. Beautiful. Roses were her favorite flower. And

Graham knew that. The cad.

Marigold watched her sniff the flower. "Do you know who sent the rose, Juliet?"

Juliet placed it back on the table and picked up her fork to continue eating. "Not really. I have a few ideas, but . . ."

Her sister smiled. "I agree with Papa. I think you know very well who sent the rose, and it does not make you happy." She tilted her head and studied her. "Although, I must say, I've seen you smile more today than I have in months."

***

Graham had decided against trying to track Juliet down by making calls at various homes that were receiving. He had no idea where she would be, and he was afraid of getting entangled in some sweet little debutante's net if he showed up at afternoon calls. Instead, he decided to ride his horse, Demon, to Hyde Park at the fashionable hour, in the hopes of seeing her there.

He had to find a way to learn her schedule so he didn't waste his time attending events where she would not be, and waiting to see if she would arrive before seeking out the next occasion for the evening. If he were to break through the barrier she had erected between them and convince her he truly wanted to marry her, he needed as much time as possible to sway her to his way of thinking.

There were many methods to persuade her, but he had to move slowly. Picking up where they'd left off was not possible, given Juliet's reaction to seeing him for the first time in months the night before.

Regardless of what she'd said, she was hurt, angry, and certainly not ready—yet—to hear him out. But what he'd shouted to her was a fact. He *would* win her back.

***

The weather was pleasant enough for an early spring day as Graham rode Demon through the gates of Hyde Park and joined the other riders and carriages travelling along the path. He stopped several times and spoke with gentlemen and ladies he hadn't seen since his return to London.

Several young ladies smiled brightly, attempted to gain his attention, and batted their eyelashes. He only had eyes for Juliet. After about fifteen minutes, a carriage rolled through the front gates with Marigold, Juliet, and two other young ladies. If he was correct, Miss Dennison and Miss Agnes Dennison were other the two.

Rather than race over to her, he took his time, circling the park, smiling, and nodding, but always aware of where her carriage was. Soon he'd held back enough that he caught up to them. "Good afternoon, ladies." He tipped his hat and smiled at the four girls.

"Good afternoon, my lord," the Misses Dennison said in unison. Marigold gave him a genuine smile of welcome. "Lord Hertford, I did not know you had returned to London." She looked at Juliet, who was gazing in the other direction. "Why did you not tell me Lord Hertford had returned?"

Juliet viewed her sister as if seeing her for the first time. "Lord Hertford?" She turned to look at him. "Oh, yes. I believe I saw him last evening."

He could not help it. All she was missing was a quizzing glass. Knowing Juliet as he did, he imagined her purchasing one to use for occasions such as this. A grin broke out on his face at her feigned indifference. Her face reddened, and he felt as though he'd scored one for his team.

"Good afternoon, Lady Juliet." He stared at her, knowing she was too well-mannered to snub him in the open with the *ton* looking on.

Her lips tightened. "Good afternoon, my lord." Then in a manner ill-suited to her normal behavior, she snapped at the driver. "May we please move forward? We are holding up the line."

The other three girls regarded her with surprise. "I'm sorry," she said, "but we were causing a traffic hold-up."

The carriage moved forward, and Graham stayed even with them. "What entertainments are you attending this evening, ladies?"

Miss Dennison related her and her sister's schedule of a dinner party and then a musicale. He turned his attention to Lady Marigold, since he knew Juliet would never tell him.

"We are attending the theater this evening, my lord. Would you care to join us?"

Juliet's groan had him biting his lip to keep from laughing. "Yes, Lady Marigold, I would love to join you. Thank you so much for your kind invitation." Before Juliet could rescind the offer, he tipped his hat once more and rode on.

He rode the pathway twice more, all the time watching Juliet pretending not to watch him. He was enjoying their little cat and mouse game.

***

Graham entered the theater lobby to see Lord Pomeroy, Lady Juliet, and Lady Marigold standing in a circle with Lord and Lady Abernathy and Mr. Applegate. He frowned at the possessive way Applegate rested his hand on Juliet's lower back. He was also standing much too close to her.

He approached the group in time for Lord Pomeroy to notice him. "Hertford, my boy, haven't seen you in a while, eh? Been hiding in the country?"

Juliet looked directly at him with a smirk on her face. No doubt wanting to see what he told her father. "Not exactly, sir. I had business that took me away from London, and then spent some time at my estate. But I am happy to be back in town for the Season."

"Good, good." He slapped him on his back. "Hope to see more of you."

"Thank you, sir." He glanced at Juliet,

pretending again to ignore him. "I intend that very thing."

A footman entered the lobby and announced the play would begin in ten minutes. The group all moved toward the stairs that would bring them to the third level where the Pomeroy box was located.

Graham gripped Applegate's shoulder, effectively stopping him, so he had to release Juliet's arm. "I say, good man, I happen to be in the market for good horseflesh. Have you been to Tattersall's lately?"

Applegate viewed him with raised brows. No doubt the man thought it was an odd time and place to have such a discussion. He cared not how crazy Applegate thought he was. He stepped around the man and took Juliet's hand and tucked her arm under his. "We will have a conversation about it, Applegate. Maybe when the play ends," he tossed over his shoulder. He leaned toward Juliet. "Good evening, Lady Juliet. I didn't get a chance to greet you before."

They started up the stairs as she spoke out of the side of her mouth. "I did not invite you, my lord, do not wish you to be here, and please release my arm."

Graham placed his hand on his chest. "You wound me, my dear. However, I did receive a lovely invitation from your charming sister."

***

Charming sister, indeed. Juliet had given Marigold

quite a dressing down over her inviting Graham to the theater with them. However, when Marigold seemed baffled by Juliet's ire over what the girl had seen as a simple invitation to a charming gentleman, Juliet snapped her mouth closed. No point in having Marigold question her further.

She and Graham had not made their courtship very well-known last Season. Not for any reason, except Juliet was afraid Papa would discourage her until Elise married. Although, truth be known, Papa was not a very strict parent, and all three girls were quite stunned when he announced his edict last year about them marrying in order of their birth.

They entered the theater box and settled into their seats. Even though Papa had invited Mr. Applegate, the man seemed to think he was there to dance attendance on her. Juliet had never been too fond of him. He stood too close, rested his hand on her back, and acted in a totally inappropriate and possessive manner, as though he had some claim on her. She hated to admit it, but she felt relief when Graham eased Mr. Applegate away from her.

Drat the man. She didn't want to be grateful to him at all.

Papa sat next to Lord and Lady Abernathy in the second row, leaving the front row open for her, Marigold, Graham, and Mr. Applegate. Since she didn't trust Mr. Applegate, she maneuvered them so he sat on the outside with her next to him—to keep him away from Marigold—with Graham next to her, and her sister at the other end.

Mr. Applegate immediately began to shift in his seat so he was closer to her. She moved so she was closer to Graham, who glanced over and immediately saw the problem. "Say, there, Applegate, how about moving over a bit. We're sort of squeezed here."

"Oh, my apologies." He moved back, annoyance written on his face. The night was certainly not starting out well. She was already irritated with the two men and the play hadn't even started.

"This is one of my favorite plays," Graham said in a low voice next to her ear. She stiffened as memories of him whispering into her ear flashed through her mind. The ache returned with a vengeance. She would not allow him to do this to her. She'd put him out of her mind, and had no intention of letting him back in again to wreak havoc on her heart.

"I hope you do not intend to disrupt the play by speaking during the performance. I prefer to enjoy the production, unlike many who come here just to socialize."

The fool man grinned at her as if he knew she was purposely attempting to antagonize him. Which, of course, was exactly what she had intended. She settled back in her seat, and studied the program.

"Have I told you how lovely you look this evening, Lady Juliet?" Mr. Applegate whispered in her other ear.

Good lord, was she to be inundated all through the play with inane comments from these two men? She took a calming breath and smiled in his direction. "Thank you very much, Mr. Applegate. Now I shall look forward to reading the program before the play starts."

Graham snorted.

She ignored him.

Mr. Applegate shifted once more to be closer to her, but rather than move near to Graham, she gritted her teeth and said nothing. Thankfully, the curtain rose, and the chatting in the audience didn't stop, but at least died down to a low murmur.

Five minutes in to the play Graham eased his hand over to her lap and covered her hand, giving it a slight squeeze. She tugged, but he held on. She tugged again. He held tighter. She leaned over toward him. "Please release my hand."

He looked at her with raised brows. "My lady, please, I am trying to listen to the actors."

She stewed in silence. Having won that round, he began to circle the inside of her wrist— which was thankfully covered by her glove—with his thumb. Despite her best efforts, her face flushed at the intimacy. She glanced sideways at him to see him studying the stage as though

41

Aristotle himself were giving a lecture.

Mr. Applegate moved his leg so his thigh pressed up against hers. Enough! She jumped up, and everyone in the box, with most likely a few across the way, looked up at her. "If you will excuse me." She made to go past Mr. Applegate.

Both men came to their feet and offered to escort her out of the box. She waved both her hands in the air like a crazy person. "No."

Papa stood. "I will escort my daughter."

By now occupants of several boxes across from them, as well as several people below were staring in her direction. Quizzing glasses and opera glasses were cast in her direction. Wonderful. Tomorrow she would be the talk of London.

Juliet turned and took her father's arm and left the box. Once they were in the lobby Papa regarded her. "Are you ill, daughter? Shall I send for the carriage?"

"No." She did want to see the play, but the distractions had become unbearable. "It was just too warm in there. I needed a breath of fresh air."

"Are you certain you are well? Lady Abernathy just mentioned she felt chilled."

"I am fine." She plastered a smile on her face. "In fact, I feel much better already. Let us return to the play."

Papa nodded and escorted her back to the box. Once they entered, she edged past Lord and Lady Abernathy and plopped down next to Papa.

With a smile of satisfaction on her face, she enjoyed the rest of the play sans distractions.

CHAPTER FOUR

After bidding farewell to Lord Pomeroy and their party, Graham climbed into his carriage and directed the driver to White's. Although not happy with the way the evening had turned out, he grinned at Juliet's maneuvers. This time he had to give the point to her. She'd managed to rid herself of both him and Applegate with quite a bit of finesse.

After she had settled behind them next to her father, Applegate had spent quite a bit of time fidgeting, looking over his shoulder at her, and glaring at him. Graham was more than happy to have had a part in ruining the man's evening, and his attempt to curry favor with Juliet.

He scowled when he thought of the man. He was much too possessive of Juliet, and needed to be put in his place very soon. Juliet was his, and no matter how much effort and time it took, he would have her. For his wife. Forever.

The ride to White's was taken up with him ruminating on his predicament and how to resolve it. If Juliet wouldn't even speak with him, it would be impossible for him to persuade her to forgive him, and let them move forward with how things had been before the duke had asked him to escort Amy to Paris.

Once again, he cursed the timing on that whole episode, but there hadn't been any way he could deny the duke's request. He just owed the man too much to turn him down. The duke had always adored his daughter, despite her deficiencies, and Graham knew the man had to have been devastated to find out she had been taken advantage of.

The time he'd spent with Amy had convinced him, however, that she had not been taken advantage of in the true sense, and indeed, did believe herself to be in love with the babe's father. Such a conundrum. When he'd left her in Paris, she was still insisting she would return to the babe's father and marry him, with or without her papa's blessing,

He'd been only too glad to be gone from that situation and let Amy's aunt deal with it.

Long-time friend, Lord Beckett, waved at him as he entered White's. Graham wended through the clusters of club members, past the betting book, and several gentlemen conversing heatedly about some measure in Parliament.

He collapsed into the comfortable chair across from Beckett.

"You're looking a bit displeased this evening." Beckett took a sip of brandy from the glass in his hand.

Graham waved at the footman to bring him a drink. "I'm afraid I've put myself into a difficult situation that will take some acumen on my part to fix." He accepted the glass from the footman and took a sip.

"A woman?"

He sighed. "What else?"

Both men pondered the state of relations between men and women for a bit. Then Beckett spoke. "What the devil have you got yourself into, anyway?"

"I was very close to offering for Lady Juliet last Season when I was unexpectedly called out of town. I sent her a note, and then a couple of letters, but it seems she hadn't received all the correspondence, or chose to ignore it. When I returned this Season, she made it perfectly clear she is finished with me." He shook his head. He sounded so pathetic he wouldn't be surprised if Beckett burst out with laughter.

"Somewhat of a pickle, eh?" Instead of laughing, he chose to take him seriously.

"My main problem is trying to spend time with her. Luckily, her sister, Lady Marigold invited me to join the family at the theater tonight. From the look on Lady Juliet's face, she was not too happy about that. But I did go, and she managed to outflank me." He grinned. "Smart girl. I was forced to admire her.

"There are many events every evening, and I

have no way of knowing where she will be."

Beckett leaned forward, dangling his glass between his knees. "You know, since I have no intention of ever succumbing to the parson's noose myself, I am more than happy to see others become besotted. M'sister, Hester, is friendly with Lady Juliet. She will undoubtedly know what events she is attending. I believe they try to meet up at these things occasionally."

"Ah. Just what I need. A spy in the enemy camp. Will she agree to a bit of espionage in the name of true love?"

"Ha! What woman does not want to see all of us lined up two-by-two like we're headed up the gangway of Noah's ark? If Hester thinks she can see another gentleman snagged, she would be thrilled." He shook his head. "Strange creatures, women are."

They pondered Beckett's acumen for a moment, staring off into space. "I'll have Hester write down the events she intends to visit with the Ladies Juliet and Marigold and send it 'round with my man. You'll have it before morning calls tomorrow."

"Be sure to impress upon Lady Hester that she is to keep her subterfuge to herself. If Lady Juliet knows there is traitor among her circle of friends, she will outwit me again."

***

The next morning, Graham studied the list of *ton* events for the next three weeks where Juliet was expected. The note had just arrived from Beckett and was more complete than he had hoped for. Among the various balls and soirees, Lady Hester had also included an accounting of to whom, and on what days, they generally made morning calls. Also catalogued were a dinner party, a garden party, and, best of all, a house party. He and Juliet under the same roof overnight brought interest to his quest and blood racing to his cock.

He checked the list against the pile of correspondence on his desk, and was pleased to see he had been invited to every event. With a quick scrawl, he accepted all the invitations, and sent them off with a messenger. Satisfied with his plan, he leaned back and smiled. The battle lines had been drawn. Today he would start his campaign in earnest.

Be aware, Lady Juliet. You are mine, and soon you will know it.

***

Juliet took a sip of her cooling tea in Miss Marshall's drawing room and nodded at Lady Pentale's running commentary on the latest gown she'd commissioned the top *modiste* in London to create for her. She went on and on about the color, the fabric, and how wonderful it would look on her. Juliet stifled a yawn, wondering how soon she and Marigold could make their escape.

"My lady, Lord Hertford," the butler announced as he stepped aside to let Graham into the room. The cad's eyes went immediately to her, and there was no doubt in her mind that he had expected to see her there.

Whatever did the man do? Travel up and down the streets of Mayfair until he'd spotted her carriage? Unfortunately, there were empty seats in the drawing room since several people had left, and one of them was right next to her. Without seeming obvious, she eased over and attempted to make it look as though the entire settee was in use.

Graham did not fall for it. He bowed to Miss Marshall to offer his felicitation, and after a few cursory comments, walked directly up to Juliet, bowed over her raised hand—drat her good manners—and with a smirk on his handsome face, eyed the seat where her gown was spread out. "May I join you, my lady?"

She swept her skirts aside. "Of course, Lord Hertford. How nice to see you." She felt as though she choked on the words, bringing a grin to his face. He settled in alongside her and accepted a cup of tea from a footman.

With shaky hands, Juliet reached for her teacup, cursing herself for slopping the tea over the brim. Once again his nearness affected her in such a frightening way. Her heart pounded, and her breathing sped up. She was finished with him, but her body did not get the message.

"Are you nervous, my lady?" Graham was all solicitations, his demeanor serious, while his eyes sparkled with hilarity. Oh, for a mere shilling she would dump the tea in his lap. The hotter, the better.

"Not at all, sir. I am merely clumsy today." Well, then. That was even worse than admitting she was nervous. She hated how the man's mere presence disturbed her.

She'd decided months ago to dismiss Lord Graham Hertford and move on to other considerations. She knew, of course, that when she did marry—whenever that would be, and certainly not to Graham—she would need to explain her lapse in judgment to her would-be betrothed before they made it final, in the event he did not wish to marry a woman no longer a virgin.

No doubt some men would withdraw their offer in that case, but there was nothing to be done for it. Since she never planned to fall in love again, one man as a husband would be as good as another. Providing he was of her class, not too old, reasonably attractive, and kind. She would enjoy a marriage of respect and fondness.

"I hope my presence is not what makes you clumsy." Graham leaned in so his words were only for her ears.

She raised her chin, but kept her voice low. "Your presence affects me in no way at all, my lord. Please do not trouble yourself that you are the reason for any distress on my part."

"Ah. Then what is the reason for your distress?"

"I am not distressed. I am very happy. Exceedingly joyful. In fact, I may burst into song at any moment."

He grinned. "Please, do."

"I may dance on the table with complete abandon, as well," she shot back. Despite her words she knew her face looked anything but cheerful. Her muscles were tight, her words sharp, and across from them, Marigold looked at her curiously.

At her last words, Graham choked on his tea and placed his cup on its saucer as he coughed until he brought himself under control. She smiled at his difficulty and took another sip of tea, turning smoothly toward Mr. Hardwick in the chair to her left. "How is your mother, Mr. Hardwick?"

"She is not well, I am afraid, Lady Juliet. She suffers from a weak constitution. It is difficult for her to come and go, and spends a great deal of time having her companion bring her drinks and such, to ease her suffering."

From what Juliet knew of Mrs. Hardwick, her only suffering she endured came from her daughter, who had gone against her wishes and married the man she loved—a solicitor—and not the titled gentleman her mother had chosen. Word was the woman was now on the prowl for the perfect wife for her son. How she would manage to do that chained to her house was a mystery.

"Please give her my regards," Juliet offered.

Their twenty minutes were up, so she stood and shook out her skirts, catching Marigold's eye. "Are you ready to depart, sister? I have a bit of shopping to do before we return home for tea."

"Ah, Lady Juliet. How fortuitous. I am headed to Bond Street, myself, and would love to treat you and Lady Marigold to an ice at Gunter's."

Juliet was about to stamp her foot. Why did she give the man that opening? She never should have said they were headed to the shops. She sighed. With everyone watching, it would be beyond rude to refuse his escort. "How charming of you to take time from your busy day to bother yourself with two silly girls on a shopping adventure, my lord. I am sure there are much more important matters to which you must attend."

Graham stood. "On the contrary. I find nothing more compelling than sharing an ice with you and your lovely sister." With a bright smile, he extended his arm toward her. Despite wishing to smack him over the head with her reticule, she managed to dredge up the semblance of a smile and took his arm.

"How very *sweet* of you, my lord." The words were bitter on her tongue as she swallowed them.

"As we arrived in a closed carriage, I am sure you realize that you cannot ride with us."

"No worries, my dear. I rode my horse, and I

will follow your carriage."

She turned as their carriage rolled up. Graham walked with them, opened the door, assisted Marigold in first, then Juliet. His hand lingered on her elbow to the point where she had to tug it free, almost falling onto the seat. She glowered at him. He gave her a bow, and turned to mount his horse.

"Juliet, why are you so mean to Lord Hertford? I thought you liked him."

She studied her sister, not sure how much to tell her. Certainly, not *everything* that had happened between them. Her face flamed at the memory. Ignoring her embarrassment, she smoothed her skirts out. "He just annoys me that is all."

"But last Season you seemed quite enamored of him. Everyone seemed so interested in Elise and St. George that it passed notice, but I thought you favored him, and expected an offer."

"La, why would you think that?" She shook her head, attempting a carefree demeanor, not sure she carried it off well, since her face still felt heated.

"You were almost rude to him last night, and then again this afternoon." Marigold grabbed the strap hanging alongside her head as the carriage turned onto Bond Street.

"Nonsense. I was not rude. And since when are you the standard bearer for my behavior?"

Marigold shrugged, ignoring her sister's tone. "I am not, and don't pretend to be. I was merely making an observation."

They both remained silent as the carriage moved in the heavy traffic. Juliet looked out the window and sucked in a breath when Graham rode by. His powerful thighs, straight back, broad shoulders and—she had to admit it—his muscular buttocks did strange things to her insides. Things she no longer wanted to feel, or think about.

The vehicle came to a stop, and the liveried footman stepped off the back and opened the door. Of course, Graham was right there, to assist her. Once she and Marigold had departed the carriage, Graham instructed her footman to see to his horse as well as the carriage.

She took his arm as they made their way to a small table outside the famous shop. He held out chairs for her and Marigold and then settled between them. Marigold seemed completely unaffected by Graham, which confused her. Why did *she* feel all these things when he was near her?

The soft breeze blew directly toward her the familiar scent of bergamot that always seemed to surround him. Her eyes teared at the memory of him holding her in his arms as they waltzed, and how safe and cared for she'd felt. Well, that was certainly a dream.

They placed their orders and chatted amiably. At least Graham and Marigold chatted. She found it hard to concentrate on anything with him so near. Chastising herself, she attempted to follow the conversation.

"So am I to understand that you do not believe in love at first sight?" Graham smiled indulgently at Marigold.

"No. I do not. It takes time for two people to learn about each other well enough to know if what they feel for each other is not merely a strong physical attraction."

Graham burst out laughing, causing Marigold to blush, but her eyes snapped.

Juliet's brows rose. "Marigold! Whatever have you been reading to say such a thing? If Papa heard you he would send you to your room to study the Bible."

Her younger sister waved her hand around. "Nonsense. I am merely disputing the 'love at first sight' of Romeo and Juliet."

"Ho! Now there's an unusual thought from a woman. I thought all women were waiting for their own true love."

"True love is built over time." Marigold sniffed. "One does not stumble into it."

Whenever had her sister developed these ideas? Juliet had been so engrossed in her own troubles that somewhere along the line Marigold had grown up. And learned things about men and women of which Papa would surely disapprove.

"Tell me, my lady," Graham directed his comment to Juliet. "What are your beliefs on love?"

Juliet hesitated. "My thoughts on love are

irrelevant, since I have learned one cannot trust love. Or perhaps I should say what one thought was love."

Graham covered her hand with his, his face losing all trace of humor. "I'm sorry you have learned that. I would like the opportunity to change your mind."

She cursed the tears that sprang to her eyes. The last thing she wanted to do was let Graham know how much he'd hurt her. She never should have answered his question, because the pain and guilt she saw in his eyes started to chip away at the solid, strong wall she'd built around her heart.

"Is something wrong that I am missing?" Marigold accepted a tart from the footman who offered her a tray of delicious looking pastries.

Juliet and Graham broke contact, and Juliet gave a soft laugh. "No, of course not. I am just fine. Those pastries look wonderful. I think I will have an apple tart." She tried very hard to hide the thickness in her voice.

Graham waved off the footman, and took a sip of his tea, his expression pensive.

Despite the tempting pastry sitting in front of her, Juliet found all she could manage was a sip of tea. Nothing else would get past the lump lodged in her throat.

CHAPTER FIVE

The Bannerman ballroom was already filled by the time Graham descended the staircase, his eyes sweeping the room for Juliet. This was one of the events on the list Lady Hester had given him.

He spotted her almost immediately. Within a circle of Lady Hester, two other ladies, and several gentlemen, she turned to regard him as his name was called. This time she didn't pretend she hadn't seen him. In fact, his heart lifted when she offered him a slight nod. Not as fine as a smile, but more than he'd gotten from her thus far.

Like a piece of metal to a magnet, he made his way to her, circling the room, his eyes never leaving hers. He practically lost his breath just watching her. She wore a pale peach gown, the neckline low enough to tantalize, but not too low to cause criticism from the matrons watching all the young ladies from their perches near the French doors.

Her golden brown hair had been swept up from her face, to cascade down her back in a riot of curls. A simple gold heart necklace surrounded her neck, the heart resting on her warm skin close to where her breasts joined. He licked his lips, remembering the pert brown nipples begging for his attention, as he'd sucked and teased, the one time he'd made love to her.

He also remembered how she threw her head back when he'd suckled hard, and panted underneath him when he slid into her moist warmth and performed the dance of lovers. She was all fire and passion, and he loved every minute of it.

He broke into a sweat.

Bloody hell, if he didn't rein in these thoughts he would not be able to finish walking up to her without calling inappropriate attention to himself.

"Good evening, ladies," he bowed in the direction of the women chatting with Juliet. They all made their curtsies. "Gentlemen," he nodded in the men's direction, trying very hard not to scowl at them.

Looking directly at Juliet, he said, "May I request a dance, my lady?"

For a moment, he thought she would refuse, but then she raised her arm and he caught the card dangling from her wrist. He wrote his name alongside a cotillion, annoyed to see all three waltzes, including the supper waltz, had been taken.

Rather than move on, he decided to stay right where he was. He wrote his name on the cards of the other ladies present, and joined in the conversation, which was mostly *ton* gossip, which he abhorred. Trying not to look conspicuous, he watched Juliet, almost certain his presence in the group disquieted her. Either that or she was coming down with an ague.

Her face was flushed, and she seemed to have trouble breathing. She let out a deep sigh and smiled when the orchestra started up a country reel and Mr. Edmond led her to the dance floor. He hated watching her dance with the man, but it would be even more difficult when she went into the arms of another man for a waltz.

He bowed to Miss Emily and offered his arm. They ended up in the line of dancers far down from Edmond and Juliet, which was probably a good thing. He would most likely make a cake of himself trying to dance the intricate steps with Miss Emily, and watch Juliet at the same time.

Although he could not hear a word Miss Emily said over the noise of the music and other conversation, nevertheless, he nodded politely, and acquiesced with a slight dip of his head when she viewed him with a questioning look. Hopefully, he hadn't agreed to something to later cause trouble. He did get a glance at Juliet and her partner, and she seemed to be having much too good of a time.

Once the dance ended, he decided it was best

if he did not subject himself to any more visions of Juliet dancing with other men. So as not to break someone's nose, he left to join those gathered in the card room until time for the rest of his dances.

He settled in, and accepted a glass of brandy from a footman. Mr. Ambrose, to his right dealt the cards. "Say, Hertford, aren't you friends with the Duke of Reading?"

"Yes. He acted as my guardian when my parents died. Why?"

"Heard he collapsed at Tattersall's two days ago. Word has it he suffered apoplexy. Hasn't turned up his toes, but supposedly he can't do much of anything."

Graham's muscles tightened. The duke had suffered apoplexy? He should visit the man. He'd been so tied into knots with Juliet, just about everything else had gone by the wayside.

Also, he wanted to see how Amy was getting on. She should have had the babe by now, and as far as Graham knew, the plan was for her to recover at her aunt's home, and then Lord and Lady Agneaux would escort her back to England.

After several hands, where he lost more than he won, he excused himself from the game and returned to the ballroom. Lady Juliet was just then returning from a dance with Lord Bennington. He joined her as Bennington left. Since none of the men had hurried to her side, he had her alone for a few minutes. If two people could be alone in a gathering of this size.

"I would like to take you driving some afternoon." He held his breath, waiting for her stinging refusal.

"Why, Graham?" She looked genuinely confused. "I've told you I have no interest in resuming our—relationship. We had our little tête-à-tête, and now that is over."

He studied her for a moment. "No, my dear. It was not merely a tête-à-tête. If you recall, I wanted to speak with your father immediately, and you told me to wait."

"Eight months?"

He ran his finger around the inside of his cravat. "As I explained, something came up that I could not avoid."

"Yet you have still not told me what it was that took you away all that time. You were at your estate, then?"

He hesitated, which Juliet did not miss, because she gave him a smirk and looked away. "Ah, I see."

Blast, this being unable to tell her the truth was trying. Well, there was nothing to be done for it. He would have to earn her trust back inch by inch. No matter how long it took, he would have her in his arms again. In his bed. In his life.

"Lady Juliet, I believe this is our dance." Mr. Davis bowed to her and extended his arm.

Without saying a word to him, she moved toward the dance floor. But not before he saw the pain and disappointment in her eyes.

***

Juliet turned toward Mr. Davis and dipped a curtsey. He took her hands in his and they began the dance. Fortunately, she'd performed these steps so many times she did not need full concentration. Instead, she dwelt on Graham. The man she'd taken months to eliminate from her mind, and heart.

If he had so easily abandoned her, why did he seem determined at this late date to take up where they'd left off? Despite his cavalier words, he certainly did not expect marriage. They had passed that point months ago. Had he sincerely wanted her for his wife, he would have found a way to see her, or visit with Papa. No, he most likely thought she was a woman of easy virtue who would engage in an affair with him.

The thought sickened her. She had to strengthen her resolve to avoid him, and concentrate instead, on the other gentlemen who wished to pay her court. Until she was safely married, Marigold could not encourage suitors, and it was not fair to her sister for Juliet to hold out.

***

Two days later, Juliet and Marigold stepped from their carriage, dressed in printed muslin afternoon gowns, with matching bonnets and parasols. Juliet had thought a picnic by the lake on the Blackmore property only ten miles, or so, outside of London would be just the thing to encourage some of the gentlemen who had been inviting her on carriage rides, sending flowers, and filling her dance card.

Since Papa's eyes had glazed over at the idea of attending a picnic, she and Marigold had arrived with Lady Osborne as their chaperone for the day, and happily joined the group under the cluster of shade trees. Benches and chairs had been set out for the guests, along with a table of lemonade and other drinks to partake before the luncheon would start.

It was doubtful Graham would attend this event. It had to have been a mere coincidence that everywhere she'd gone so far, he'd been there. So many parties, balls, and other occasions were held each day that the chances of them running into each other was slight, unless planned.

Many of the men she'd been flirting with asked each evening where she would be the next day, but Graham never asked. He merely showed up. Strange, that.

She twirled her parasol and flirted with Mr. Davis and Mr. Edmond. Both had sent her flowers that morning, and both would be considered acceptable husbands. Neither had a title, as the second and third sons of earls. However, titles did not impress her, and the men were both handsome and wealthy in their own right. She could certainly do worse.

Except each of them had stolen a kiss, and she was disappointed that she'd felt nothing. In fact, Mr. Edmond's kiss was simply boring. Not at all like the excitement she'd felt when . . .

Her twirling parasol and wandering thoughts both stopped abruptly as Graham came into view. For heaven's sake, how did he manage to turn up at this event, too? His grin as he spotted her and headed in her direction only annoyed her further. She would never be able to put him from her mind, and concentrate on finding a husband, if he kept showing up and distracting her.

The man was a nuisance.

"Good afternoon, Lady Juliet." Graham bowed and regarded her with a slight grin. Oh, if she weren't so flustered at his presence, she would love to remove that arrogant smirk from his handsome face. Her hand itched to do just that. But she would never let him know she cared one whit about him being here.

"My lord," she mumbled in her best bored manner, and dipped her head.

Why did the man have to look so good? And why after Mr. Edmond and Mr. Davis had held her attention for a good part of an hour, she now could not concentrate on anything they said?

"'Tis a lovely day for a picnic, is it not?"

Confounded it, and blast, since the sun shone brightly for the first time in days, she would be forced to agree with him, or else look like a fool. "Yes, my lord. A lovely day, indeed."

She turned to Mr. Davis. "I understand there is a charming path through the wooded area on the south side of the estate. I would love to see it."

Mr. Davis fell all over himself answering that he would love to escort her there. Thinking she had solved the problem of Graham, she smiled and took his arm. Except both Mr. Edmond and Graham agreed a walk in the woods was the very thing, and they would join them as well. They proceeded to follow behind them, like baby ducks trailing their mother.

She sighed, reconciled to having Graham addle her thoughts. It had been ridiculous to think they would not want to join them, but at least he was behind her.

Watching her walk.

She groaned, remembering Graham telling her last Season the view of her walking ahead of him was a wonderful sight, indeed. She blushed at the memory and tried very hard to keep her hips steady.

A heavy hand landed on Mr. Davis's shoulder. "I say, Davis, was that you I saw at Tattersall's last week?" Graham's comment effectively stopped her and Mr. Davis as the man considered if he had been at Tattersall's. He turned slightly toward Graham to answer him, dropping her arm from where she held his. Graham stepped up, took hold of her arm, and moved them forward. "Probably not. Must have been someone who looked like you," he tossed over his shoulder.

Looking thoroughly confused, Mr. Davis opened his mouth to speak, and then shut it a couple of times, looking much like a fish. Shaking his head, he fell in alongside Mr. Edmond, behind Graham and Juliet as the walk continued.

Juliet hissed from the side of her mouth "That was not well done. And that same line is getting old. How many times do you intend to waylay my partners with the ridiculous question about Tattersalls?"

"As many times as it takes to make sure you do not encourage other gentlemen when you belong to me."

She gritted her teeth. "Oh, your arrogance is unparalleled. I do not belong to you. And I specifically inquired if Mr. Davis would escort me on a walk. I did not invite you, nor do I wish to be partnered with you."

Graham leaned in. "Hush, sweeting. You don't want the other gentlemen to think you rude."

To her absolute horror, he winked at her.

***

Graham loved when Juliet was rattled. It meant he was winning. Had she been indifferent to his comments and nearness, he'd be worried. After his maneuvering to get her next to him, her face was flushed, and her chest heaving, but he was sure this time in anger. Most likely she wanted more than anything to smack him over the head with her parasol. Too much a lady.

The four wandered the path in silence until Mr. Edmond began to point out different trees and flora. Unfortunately, he must have considered himself somewhat of an expert because he used all the Latin terms, which no one else seemed to understand. His comments were met with a whole lot of, '*ah,*' and '*indeed,*' as well as nodding of heads.

Graham needed to get Juliet alone to make any headway with her. Convincing her he was serious about marriage, and had no intention of disappearing ever again, would not be possible with a crowd around them.

"Look, a creek!" Juliet pointed to a small brook running through the area. "Oh, I would so like to walk across it." She turned to him, probably forgetting she was trying to ignore him.

"So, we shall." He steered her in the direction of the swiftly moving water.

"I say, old man, I don't think we should try to cross. The water looks rather menacing for a young lady." Mr. Edmond viewed the creek with furrowed brows.

"Oh, I shall be fine, Mr. Edmond. My sisters and I walked across brooks many times. There is a certain knack to it, you know." She released his arm, and studied the water. Slowly she followed the water's edge, going several yards downstream, the men trailing behind. "There! See, there are stones almost in a row right across the water."

"Um, I don't think you should try walking on those stones. Maybe find an easier place to cross?" Although he had agreed, mostly to gain her favor, Graham was beginning to think this was not such a good idea, after all.

"Don't be silly." She waved her parasol in the air. "I have this to balance me."

Bloody hell, did she see herself as a circus performer? "Ah, no."

She turned to him, her face flushed. "You cannot tell me what to do, Lord Hertford." Despite referring to him by his title was the proper thing to do with Edmond and Davis present, it still stung to hear her address him so formally.

Juliet stepped on the first stone and Graham grabbed her hand. She tried to shake it off, but he held firm, until she tugged. "Stop, I can do this." She took two more steps and turned to smile at them just as her foot slipped. Wobbling back and forth, parasol waving in the air, she yelped and fell face first into the water.

"Lady Juliet!" all three men shouted. While the other two dimwits just stared at her, their mouths agape, Graham grabbed her by the arms and pulled her up. She gasped and began to sputter and cough.

He bent her over his arm at the waist and patted her back as she continued to drag in breaths, cough, and sputter. "Stay calm, you will be all right."

After a few minutes her breathing slowly evened out.

Graham swung her into his arms and strode from the creek, with other two men continuing to stare at them open-mouthed. Idiots.

"What…what are you doing?" She still found it hard to speak without coughing.

"I'm taking you home. You are soaked to the skin, and even though it is sunny, you cannot stay here in the air."

"Fine." She coughed again. "But there is no need to carry me."

He starred at her, his lips tight. He never should have allowed her to do such a foolish thing. "You can't even talk without coughing, how are you going to walk back to the carriages?"

Cough. "I can manage."

Graham snorted and continued, with the two useless men following them. He shifted her to get a better grip. "Put your arms around my neck."

She shook her head. "My lord," she coughed, "you do not need," she coughed again, "to hold me like this. And please move your hands."

"I cannot move my hands without dropping you."

"Graham, my skirts are dragging, and my legs are showing!" She choked as she tried to wiggle, most likely to have him put her down. "If we arrive back at the picnic like this, I will be ruined." A long string of coughs followed her lengthy speech.

He shifted her body, pulling her against his chest. "Fix them."

"For heaven's sake, just put me down." She fumbled with the skirts, and got them to cover her legs. "There is no need to carry me."

"Your shoes are wet. If I allow you to walk, you will slip and slide all over the grass."

A few more coughs. "It is not your responsibility to *allow* me to do anything. I am not your concern."

"Yes, you were once my concern, you are now, and always will be."

She huffed and crossed her arms over her breasts, making it almost impossible to carry her. "I told you to put your arms around my neck or I will drop you."

"There is no need to carry—"

There was only one way to shut her up. He lowered his head, and his mouth covered hers. At first she resisted his kiss, then her lips softened, and rather than walk into a tree with his attention taken up with Juliet's warm, moist mouth, he came to a stop.

Her arms finally encircled his neck.

"Ah, Lord Hertford, I don't think it is quite proper to be kissing Lady Juliet in the open like this," Mr. Davis said from behind them.

Graham pulled his mouth away from hers, immediately regretting the loss of her sweetness. "Bugger off, Davis, and run ahead and ask for my phaeton to be brought around. And take that other idiot with you."

Davis and Edmond looked affronted, but did as he bid and hurried ahead.

"I beg of you, Graham, for the sake of my reputation, can you please put me down? You can hold my arm so I can walk, but this is inappropriate. It's bad enough Mr. Davis and Mr. Edmond witnessed this, but there are many of the worst gossips in the *ton* down there." Her eyes pleaded with him.

Realizing what she said was true, he released her legs so her feet hit the ground. He put his arm out, and she took it. When her wet slippers started to slip on the damp grass, he placed his arm around her waist.

At her glare, he said, "Don't try to dissuade me from holding you Juliet. If you fall again you could hurt yourself."

Dripping wet and clinging to him, she nodded briefly as they made their way over the hill toward the gathering.

CHAPTER SIX

Juliet was no longer dripping, but still quite wet when she and Graham entered her townhouse. Despite her objection, he insisted on driving her home in his phaeton, which he pointed out was certainly proper since it was an open vehicle. Not wanting to spoil the fun for Marigold, she agreed so the carriage could stay there to bring her and Lady Osborne back when the picnic ended.

He gave her his jacket to wear, and wrapped her legs with a blanket he kept in the vehicle. Sitting so close to him as he drove her home was disconcerting. She needed to avoid him if she were to have any peace of mind.

"I believe I asked once before if I may take you on an afternoon ride through the park. Can we set a time this week?" He glanced sideways at her, a certain hopefulness in his eyes.

She pulled the sides of his jacket closer, annoyed at the scent of him on the garment, but the slight breeze from the ride chilled her, so she had no choice. "Very well, since I don't believe you will stop asking. However, I beg you not to read too much into it. I must marry this Season so Marigold can have her chance next year. 'Tis Papa's edict."

His lips tightened, and his eyes snapped. "I have told you my plans for us include marriage. You seem to be under the illusion that I want something nefarious from you." He switched the reins to his right hand and covered her hands fisted in her lap with his warm hand. "Not so, sweeting, I do not want you for an affair, I want you for my wife."

"I don't trust you." The whispered words barely made it past her lips.

His head jerked. "What?"

She cleared her throat. "I said, I don't trust you. You still have not told me to where you disappeared. How do I know you will not do so again?"

"Juliet, I promise you, what took up my time has nothing to do with us. I would never do anything to hurt you." He studied her, leaving her feeling like a bug under glass. "If it takes the rest of the Season, I will earn your trust back. Just promise me you will not accept any other suitors until I've had my chance."

She turned from the piercing look in his eyes to gaze out at the snug, well-tended lawns in front of the townhouses they passed. She wanted so much to believe him. But her heart kept reminding her that it was still newly healed. Did she want to put herself through that agony again?

***

"Is it raining so hard?" Papa asked as he walked down the corridor, staring at them over the top of his spectacles, an open book in his hand. "Funny, the last time I looked it was quite sunny."

"No, Papa, I fell in the brook at the picnic." She sneezed, then smiled warmly at him. Despite his totally unexpected edict about them all marrying in order of their birth, he was such a dear.

"Picnic, you say? Yes, yes, I remember, Lady Osborne went with you. Dreadful things, picnics." He frowned. "Where was your chaperone when you were playing in the water?"

"I wasn't playing, Papa, I fell." Honestly, sometimes he acted as though she and Marigold were still young girls needing constant supervision.

Well, perhaps she did, on occasion.

She glanced at Graham, who was grinning widely. "Lady Juliet attempted to cross the brook while stepping on stones, and she tumbled into the water."

"Ah, my sweet daughter, the light of my life. How many times have I told you not to do that?"

Her lips tightened at his reprimand, especially when Graham choked back a laugh. "That is precisely what I told her, sir."

Papa looked at Graham, as if noting his presence for the first time. "Hertford, is it not?"

Graham straightened as if commanded. "Yes, sir."

Papa's eyes narrowed. "Weren't you dancing around my daughter last year?"

Now she choked back a laugh at the uncomfortable look on Graham's face.

"Sir, I believe you could say Lady Juliet and I spent some time together."

"Good, good." He turned to Juliet. "My dear, I think you should go change to avoid an ague." He nodded toward Graham. "Join me in my library, Hertford. I could use a cup of tea." He slapped Graham on the back, effectively moving him down the corridor, leaving him no choice.

Juliet climbed the stairs to her bedchamber. She rang for Charlene to help her out of her clothes and bring a hot bath. The damp clothes were giving her a chill, and the bath would be just the thing.

She was a little concerned about Papa inviting Graham for tea. First of all, Papa never drank tea outside of their regular tea in the afternoon, and most times he wasn't at home for that. Second, she did not like the look in his eyes when he slapped Graham on the back and practically pushed him to the library.

The last thing she wanted was Papa whipping out marriage contracts and Graham confessing that was what he wanted. Even if she did believe him that he was truly interested in marriage, and not simply an affair, she wasn't sure that was best for her.

There was no doubt Graham could bring her incredible happiness, but then he could also take it away. Vulnerability was a terrible thing, she'd learned. There was no other way to state it than he'd broken her heart. It had taken her months to feel whole again, and she was not about to open herself up to heartache again.

***

"Here, my boy, have a seat." Lord Pomeroy waved to a comfortable chair near the fireplace. He walked to the bell pull and yanked. He waited patiently by the door until a footman appeared and he ordered tea and sandwiches.

Rubbing his hands together, he joined Graham in the chair opposite the small table between them. "So. A Marquess, correct?"

"Yes, sir."

"Lady Juliet is a lovely girl. Kind, patient, cares for children. She doesn't run the house as well as her sister did, but she tries hard."

Graham tried very hard to not laugh out loud. It was obvious what Pomeroy was doing, and he couldn't help but imagine how outraged Juliet would be to listen to her father tout all her good points when she was trying to discourage him.

"I agree. Lady Juliet is truly a treasure."

The man's face lit up. "Yes, yes. I adore all my daughters, you know. My eldest, Lady St. George only married last year. Happy as lovebirds, those two. Does my heart good. They've already added a babe to the family." He stopped speaking when the footman entered with a full tray. After placing it in front of the two men, he left the room.

Pomeroy poured tea for them both, that Graham fixed it to his liking, then placed a couple of small sandwiches and a miniscule pastry on a plate. Since he'd missed luncheon at the picnic, he was quite hungry. Of course, carrying a soaking wet Juliet had also increased his appetite. He laughed to himself. Increased his appetites in more ways than one.

Graham enjoyed his food while waiting for Pomeroy to continue enumerating Juliet's qualities. Graham, of course, could also throw in passionate, adventurous, and innocently enthusiastic in the bedchamber, but since he assumed he was a better shot than Pomeroy, he didn't want to make Juliet an orphan.

Pomeroy wiped his mouth with his serviette and leaned back. "Yes, my boy, Juliet is one fine young woman. Would make someone a spectacular wife." He leaned forward as if imparting a great secret. "Had to light a fire under my eldest last year, or she would never have married. Told them all they had to marry in order of their birth. Scared the living daylights out of Lady St. George. She never intended to wed, hoped to spend her life a spinster, organizing gatherings for strange people, and directing my life."

So, that was why he'd made that edict to which Juliet had referred. As much as Pomeroy seemed to love his daughters, he obviously wanted some freedom from their directing. Yes, he could imagine having three grown daughters attempting to make life comfortable for him by arranging it precisely the way young ladies thought life for a gentleman should be.

The complete opposite of how a man wanted his life to be. Especially when he'd already done his job as a father, and was nowhere near his dotage.

"I will be honest with you, sir. I have a great deal of respect for Lady Juliet, and hope to spend more time with her over the next few weeks." All things considered, he didn't dare get more formal than that.

Pomeroy beamed. Graham could almost see him mentally checking his schedule to see where he could fit in a consultation with a wedding planner. That would be fine with him. Right now, there were simply too many men interested in Juliet.

She was his.

"I'm glad to hear that. If there's anything I can do to move it along, my boy, let me know."

He would love to have a push from Pomeroy, but the better side of caution prevailed. He would do well to give Juliet time, and woo her as he had before. Apparently, from Pomeroy's attitude, he had no notion of the disappointment Juliet had suffered after he had absconded last year.

Pomeroy frowned and looked at him. "Do you like this women's food?" He waved at the tray of tea and sandwiches, cut so expertly into crust-less squares and triangles. "My daughters tell me it is good for my health. I think it's good for infants with no teeth."

Graham choked back a laugh. How did one answer that question when one was a guest in the man's home?

"Tell you what, Hertford. Let's have a brandy, and then ride on down to White's where we can get something substantial to eat. Something that requires chewing." He jumped up and strode to the sideboard, pouring them both a healthy portion of brandy.

If this was the type of fare that came from the kitchen, Graham was beginning to see exactly why Pomeroy was anxious to see his daughters married. He had indulged in several of the little sandwiches and was still hungry.

He accepted the glass from Pomeroy, who held it up. "To daughters. May you have many, and live to see them all married and settled in their own homes, directing their husbands' and children's lives." He downed the brandy in one gulp. "Now let's see about getting something decent to eat."

***

The next afternoon as Graham rode his horse to the Duke of Reading's home, he mused on the time spent with Juliet's father the day before. He found the man entertaining, extremely fond of his daughters, but determined to see them set up in their own homes.

He had every intention of removing Juliet from under his care. At least forming a bond with Lord Pomeroy had helped. He only hoped it did not antagonize Juliet. As her father had rightly pointed out, she had numerous good qualities, but he had also found her to be stubborn, headstrong, and determined. Fine qualities also, if they weren't in the path of his own purposes.

The man at the duke's door accepted his card and asked that he wait in the drawing room. He followed him upstairs and settled in, waiting to be summoned. Unable to sit, with concerns on how he would find the duke, he wandered the room, memories flooding back from his time spent here.

Once he'd been placed under the duke's care, following the fire, he'd been sent directly to this townhouse. Even though he'd seen the duke over the years, he was still practically a stranger when the thirteen-year-old boy arrived.

He'd been at school when the fire erupted, burning their London townhouse to the ground and killing his parents. Once the funeral at Hertford Manor was over, he and the duke, along with Amy, traveled to the duke's estate in Suffolk, where Graham had remained for the rest of the school term that year. Although he had expected to return to Eton when the new term began, the duke decided to keep him at the estate and take his lessons with Amy until he was ready for university. Given how much time the duke had spent in counseling and preparing Graham for his responsibilities, it was the best thing he could have done for his ward.

The Duchess of Reading had not been too fond of having Graham 'underfoot' as she put it, but the duke was adamant that Graham needed time to prepare for his new life. Always embarrassed and irritated by her 'different' daughter, the duchess spent her time in London, or in Bath. Rarely did she join the family in Suffolk. In fact, Graham only remembered her visiting them at Christmastide each year. The visit would last for only a few days before she again left in a flurry of goodbyes, kisses on her daughter's head, and a light peck from the duke on her cheek.

He'd always felt sorry for the duke, since he was such a pleasant man, devoted to his daughter, and serious in his responsibilities to his title. But their marriage, like most in the *ton*, had been arranged for purposes of money, power, and solidifying relationships. However, everyone, including the staff, seemed to breathe a sigh of relief when the duchess departed and life resumed its normal pattern.

His thoughts were interrupted by the return

of the butler. "My lord, if you will follow me, the duke will see you now."

Graham followed him down a long corridor, and up another flight of stairs to the floor where the private family suites were located. He could smell the sick room before he entered. The room was dark, the drapes drawn, even though the day was bright and cheery. He never understood the doctors' dictates that the sick room must be kept overwarm and dark.

The great Duke of Reading rested on his back, looking shrunken in the huge bed. As Graham grew closer, he noticed one side of his face drooped, as well as one eyelid. His breathing was so shallow for a moment Graham thought he had expired. "Your Grace?"

He opened his eyes, offering a crooked smile, a slight bit of moisture dripping from the side of his mouth. He reached his hand out and Graham took it. Despite his illness, his grip was still as strong and firm as he'd remembered.

The duke tried to speak, but only garbled words came out. There was an attendant there in the room with him. Graham turned to him. "Do you know what he said?"

"'Tis hard to understand His Grace, and sometimes he gets quite frustrated. However, he can write words since 'tis the left side of his body affected, and he is right-handed. Do you wish me to procure some vellum and a pen?"

"Yes, please."

Graham pulled up a chair and sat next to the duke. "Your attendant is getting writing materials for you."

His Grace nodded his head, and continued to grip his hand. He'd known people who had suffered apoplexy, two had died before regaining consciousness, and the other one had lingered for weeks in the same condition as the duke.

He was reluctant to ask about the duchess, but with Amy not able to take care of matters, the poor man was left with no family to help. Graham decided to speak with the duke's solicitors in the next few days to make sure all was in order.

The attendant returned with the vellum and a pen. The duke released Graham's hand and began to write. His writing was clear and precise. He finished and held the document out to him.

Take care of Amy.

"I will, Your Grace. Have no fear. I will see that she is well taken care of."

One lone tear trickled down the man's face to pool at this mouth. Despite his reluctance to do so, Graham was forced to ask. "Has Her Grace been notified?"

The duke waved his good arm around, and sprouted words totally inaudible, his face growing red with anger. Graham looked toward his attendant with a frown.

"Her Grace was notified the day it happened, my lord. She sent a note that she was quite distraught and would come for a visit in a few weeks, when she felt more at ease."

Blasted, bloody hell.

Even if she didn't love the man, he was her husband of many years, and he had been good to her. She also had a vulnerable daughter with no parent to look out for her welfare.

The duke appeared to have exhausted himself with Graham's visit, so he leaned over the bed and said, "I will leave now, but rest assured I will see that all is taken care of for Amy."

He nodded and closed his eyes.

As Graham stepped out of the room, the butler waited on the other side. "My lord, Lady Amy has requested you join her in her sitting room."

In his pursuit of Juliet, he wasn't aware that Amy had returned from Paris, but he would be glad to see her. He followed the man once again to the other end of the corridor to Amy's rooms. She sat on the padded window seat, staring out at the garden. The last time he'd seen her, she was several months pregnant, but now she was back to her slender self. She turned from the window as he entered.

Before he took even one step, she ran across the room, and threw herself into his arms. She immediately burst into tears, clinging to his jacket, her slender body shaking with sobs. He put his arm around her and led her to the settee. He reached into his pocket and pulled out a handkerchief and handed it to her. "Here, poppet."

She felt so much smaller, and fragile than when he'd seen her last. Then she'd been rounder. Once her tears subsided, he put his knuckle under her chin and raised her face to look at her. "What is wrong, Amy? Is it your father? I will see that you are taken care of."

She shook her head and twisted the handkerchief in her hands. "No. Papa is not well. I am so sad for that, but something else hurts me even more."

He brushed the strands of hair back from her face. "What is it, sweeting?"

Tears slowly fell from her eyes once more, rolling down her cheeks, dropping onto her lap. "I want my baby. They took it away."

CHAPTER SEVEN

Juliet and Marigold climbed into their carriage, settling on one side of the comfortable coach. Lady Selina Crampton, whom Papa had secured as a combination companion and chaperone for the rest of the Season, took the seat opposite them, adjusting her skirts. He'd introduced her to them the week before, citing again his wish for Juliet to find a husband this Season, and his dislike of too many *ton* events to continue as their chaperone.

Juliet did not the look in Papa's eyes when he mentioned her getting married. He'd been acting strangely happy around her ever since Graham's visit. She'd even heard him whistling in the corridor as he went about his business. Hopefully, Papa had not already given his consent to Graham's request for her hand. At one time that would have made her ecstatic, now she wasn't sure how she would feel about it.

Lady Crampton was a charming woman, a widow of perhaps five and thirty years, the mother of two young daughters. Juliet hadn't asked, but for some reason she thought Papa was paying the woman for her services. Which, of course, could create a scandal for her, and her daughters.

Widows who accepted money from a gentleman were immediately considered a mistress. Which was probably why Papa introduced her as a companion. That was an acceptable type of employment, if not an enviable one.

However, there was something about this woman that refuted any ideas of impropriety. Lady Crampton was pretty in an older woman sort of way, with bright hazel eyes, beautiful skin, and a lovely smile that warmed up the room. Her manners were impeccable, and she was a stickler for decorum.

She had arrived at their home with her two daughters in tow, in an elegant, but outdated, afternoon gown and pelisse. Papa had insisted if she were to assume the duties of chaperone and companion in a successful manner, it would be necessary for her to take up residence in their home. So, the nursery was re-opened, where two adorable twin girls, Lady Phoebe and Lady Prudence, two and ten years, had been installed. Which, of course, required a governess for them.

Within days of Lady Crampton's arrival boxes began to appear that were sent directly to her bedchamber. Apparently, part of the pay for her services included a new, updated wardrobe.

When Juliet thought on the entire matter, it did seem unusual to go through all that trouble to hire a chaperone, but Papa had some odd ways about him, so she shrugged it off.

The carriage rolled down the pathway as they headed to the Colborne house party. Their home was only about a four-hour ride from London, so Cook had packed a luncheon for them to enjoy on the road, rather than having to stop at an inn for a meal.

Juliet had been looking forward to the party for some time now. She preferred the country to Town life, even though it was a necessity to be in London for the Season. Papa took up his Parliamentary duties, and she and her sisters attended events that would expose them to proper gentlemen with the goal of marriage.

Once they were well into the Season, she always found herself longing for their estate in Hampshire. The fresh air, the smell of grass and sunshine, she and her horse, Peony, racing over the grounds. Of course, there would be no opportunity to race over the grounds at the Colborne house party, since she preferred aside in her breeches when riding at home.

She stared out the window as they left London proper and entered the outskirts of the town. Her mind wandered back to the conversation Graham and her father had several days ago when she returned home drenched from her fall in the creek.

In fact, she'd been horrified when the sound of male voices had come from the entrance hall. She hurried down the corridor to see Papa and Graham leaving together, both seeming to have a most friendly relationship.

Although not impertinent enough to flat out ask Papa what they had discussed, she hinted several times, but he always smiled his favorite ambiguous smile and repeated what an upstanding young man the Marquess of Hertford was.

And then he began to whistle again.

Would that upstanding young man be at the house party? Given how often he'd appeared at events she'd attended, there was little doubt in her mind that he would pop up at the house party. How would she handle being under the same roof as Graham? The last time they'd attended a house party together, they'd ended up in the same bed.

And months of misery had been her penance.

***

After the four-hour drive, their carriage meandered along a lengthy driveway, through acres of lovely, well-tended lawns and gardens, before the coach drew up to the front of Colborne Hall. Lady Charlotte walked with her mother, Lady Colborne, down the graveled path from the front door to greet Juliet, Marigold, and Lady Crampton.

"Lady Crampton, I am so pleased you are

able to join us. I was thrilled when I received Lady Juliet's note that you are now serving as companion and chaperone to the girls. It has been years since we've spoken." Lady Colborne took both of Lady Crampton's hands in hers, smiling brightly.

Apparently, their chaperone and Lady Colborne had been good friends at one time, although Lady Crampton had not mentioned that when Juliet had told her about the house party.

"Yes, I am so very happy to be here. It has been much too long. I'm afraid I have become somewhat of a recluse since his lordship's death." Lady Crampton did not seem as distraught as one would think if she had hidden herself away after her husband's death.

Lady Charlotte linked her arm in Juliet's. "This party is going to be ever so much fun. I have all sorts of games planned, as well as a picnic." She leaned in, lowering her voice. "Mother has invited a number of eligible men who have all accepted." Her blush had Juliet wondering if one particular man was of interest to her hostess.

She'd heard rumors that Lady Charlotte had been happily courted by Mr. Cecil Moore, a second son of an Earl. Apparently, the charming man without a title, however, had not impressed her father as suitable for his only daughter. There were so many times that she hated the strictures of their life. Far too many members of the *ton* did not believe love and marriage were compatible, or even necessary.

Although tempted to ask if another certain eligible man had been invited and accepted, she decided it would be better to just wait and see. There had been some gossip when Graham, who had been viewed as courting Juliet last Season, suddenly left London.

Charlotte took Marigold's arm in hers, and they sauntered up to the front door, with Lady Crampton and Lady Colborne following them, chatting merrily away.

***

Graham waved his valet away. "That's fine. If you keep this up, I will be viewed as a fop."

Carson huffed at being dismissed before he felt his master looked acceptable, by his own high standards. He bent to begin cleaning up from Graham's bath.

Graham was more concerned with joining the others at the house party before Juliet was swamped by the numerous young bucks in attendance. He'd seen Lords Blakely and St. Clair, along with Mr. Gibbons as he had arrived earlier. From what he knew, they were all looking for wives this Season.

Blakely and St. Clair needed heirs, and Gibbons needed a healthy dowry. That thought brought a smile to his face, remembering his lunch with Lord Pomeroy. There was no doubt in his mind that Pomeroy had been sizing him up as a husband for Juliet, and had not found him wanting. That, at least, was one hurdle gotten over.

Now to convince the young lady that marriage to him would be a wise decision for her. He left his assigned bedchamber and headed downstairs to the drawing room where the guests were gathering before dinner.

Sure enough, Juliet, along with Lady Charlotte and Lady Marigold, was surrounded by several gentlemen, all of them vying for their attention. Although, it appeared to him they were more interested in gaining Juliet's favor than the other two ladies. Not in a mood to appear like a young pup in love by competing with the others, he moved toward a footman holding a tray of drinks and chose a glass of sherry.

In love.

Yes, that about covered it. He was in love with Juliet and had every intention of once again gaining her trust so she would agree to marry him. It hadn't taken him long after his trip with Amy before he started to realize he not only wanted Juliet for his marchioness, he was in love with her. Besotted was the term that came to mind, in fact.

Amy was another conundrum he needed to deal with. He'd been stunned to hear her say she wanted her baby back because 'they' took it. He'd never spoken to her about the child because the duke had claimed it had all been arranged. She would stay with her aunt in Paris until the babe as born, when it would be brought to a foundling home, and Amy would return to England.

From what Amy had stated to him in between sobs, no one had ever told her that would happen. She was devastated when the babe was taken from her, and she was whisked away to a house along the French coast to recover from the birth. Any questions about the babe were answered with a pat on her head and assurance that all would be fine.

He'd always resented how everyone except him and the duke had treated the girl as if she were a child. Certainly, she had many childlike ways about her, and her maturity level had never reached full adulthood, but she was not stupid. She understood a lot more than anyone gave her credit for.

Amy was also a sweet, happy, loving young woman. Seeing her in the state she was in when he'd visited the duke had crushed him. He promised he would speak with her father on her behalf, but with him barely hanging onto life, that would be a tricky business, at best.

He had also been quite surprised to discover she claimed to be in love with the man who had fathered her baby. She refused to name him, but he had to have been someone who worked on her father's estate. She had insisted he loved her and wanted to take care of her and the baby. How much of that was wishful thinking, he had no idea, but it was something he was bound by his allegiance to the duke to figure out.

But now he had to concentrate on his own situation. As she sipped his sherry and considered what his next move should be, a butler appeared at the door to the drawing room to announce dinner.

As a marquess, Graham was near the head of the line into dinner, escorting Lady Thorne, the Earl of Thorne's wife. He was behind them, escorting Lady Charlotte. They entered the dining room, the table extending quite a way down the room, with seating for the sixty or so guests at the party.

The whispered words he had uttered into his hostess's ear upon his arrival had paid off, and Juliet was seated to his right. Better to attempt to woo her at the dining table, then to fight the crowd of men who had surrounded her earlier.

"Good evening, my lady. I hope your journey was uneventful?" He was already feeling the effects of her being so near. The wonderful scent of lilacs surrounding her, along with the warmth from her body, had his blood pumping, and not to the best place while in company. But on the other hand, he could not get enough of her.

"Yes, it was quite an ordinary trip. Only a few hours, so it was not necessary for us to stop, except to change horses and refresh ourselves. Did you find your trip pleasant?"

"I did. Although I imagine my trip was

quieter than yours. I see you have a new chaperone?" He nodded further down the table at Lady Crampton.

She followed his glance. "Yes, father secured the services of Lady Crampton for the rest of the Season. She is acting as companion and chaperone for myself and Marigold."

"I know her from my relationship with Lord Crampton. He and I were on the same committee in Parliament a couple of years ago. A strange man. Somewhat older than his wife. A quiet sort. Never spoke much about his family. From what I learned he married Lady Crampton in the hopes of securing a spare to his heir who he'd fallen out with."

Juliet laughed. A wonderful sound after so many terse exchanges between them. "Lady Crampton has two daughters. Twins. Beautiful little girls. They've taken up residence in the nursery, and already have Cook wrapped around their fingers." She glanced down the table at the woman. "We are happy to have her. She is most pleasant, and I am sure will keep us out of trouble." She glanced sideways at him, a smirk on her face.

Suddenly, he remembered the last house party they'd attended together. Yes, having Lady Crampton keeping an eye on things would be best. For Juliet, anyway.

He, of course, had other ideas.

***

Juliet couldn't help but relish the look on Graham's face. It was enjoyable to see the disappointment when she'd mentioned how Lady Crampton would allow no impropriety here. There were other couples, she knew from past experience, who would be wandering the halls once everyone had retired for the night. Every house party had those few.

She had no intention of letting Graham anywhere near her bedchamber. Since she was sharing with Marigold, unlike last year when she'd had her own room at the Grantham house party, it would not be possible for him to visit her room, anyway.

"I understand Lady Charlotte has games planned for this evening. Will you be joining in, or do you intend to seek out the room where card tables are being set up?" Juliet took a sip of her wine, studying him over the rim.

Annoyed at the reaction her body was having to his proximity, she hoped he would go off with the other gentlemen and play cards. Then she wished he wouldn't, and cursed her prevaricating. He still threw her emotions into turmoil. She so much wanted to simply dismiss him as a cad and a bounder, and set her sights on some of the other gentlemen.

Even at this party, there were several pleasant looking men, some with titles, some without, most with wealth, a couple without. Certainly, from this crowd, there had to be one or two who would make her heart beat fast and her breathing to increase like Graham did. Except during the entire Season thus far that had not happened.

Then she quickly reminded herself she did not want those feelings. That was what led her down the path to disgrace last year.

"No, I think I will spend time with the group playing games. As much as I enjoy cards, I can do that anytime." He leaned in close. "I'm hoping you and I can partner in a game or two. If I remember correctly, we did quite well last year in charades."

"Indeed we did. If memory serves, you were adept at giving out clues, and I excelled in guessing."

Graham studied her for a minute, his face serious. "We are a good team, are we not, sweeting?"

Juliet sucked in a breath at his intimate comment, and looked around, but no one seemed to be paying attention to them. "You overstep yourself, my lord."

He bowed his head. "I apologize if I caused you discomfort." He took a sip of wine, then said, "But my observation stands on its own merits."

The first course of turtle soup, oyster pate, lamb cutlets, asparagus with peas, and other items were already on the table. Graham offered her the various dishes, and then filled his own plate. A turbot with lobster and Dutch sauce was carved on the sideboard, and offered to each guest by a footman.

The meal passed pleasantly, with Juliet conversing with both Graham on her left and Mr. Ambrose on her right. He was an older man, looking for a wife, rumor had it. Apparently, he was at a loss as to how to raise his two daughters. He complained about lax governesses, tears and wailing from his daughters, and the formidable task of getting them married, even though they were only ten and eleven years. His somber expression, and constant grumblings about daughters in general, and his in particular, soon had her spending most of her time speaking with Graham.

Her own papa had done a fine job of raising her and her two sisters after their mother had passed away. She had been only six years at the time, Marigold only five. Her elder sister, Elise, had taken over the mother duties, even though she had only been ten years herself.

Being so young when her mother died, Juliet hadn't remembered her too much. It seemed in her mind Mama was a tall woman, who was soft when she held her on her lap, and smelled of lemons.

Once the dinner had ended, Lady Colborne stood and invited the ladies to join her in the drawing room for tea and conversation while the gentlemen enjoyed their port. Juliet stood as Graham drew out her chair. He leaned in and said, "I would like a walk with you in the gardens later. Would that be acceptable?"

Juliet hesitated, her heart beginning to pound. Alone with Graham in the gardens? Most likely not a good idea, but on the other hand, she had a feeling he would not discontinue his pursuit of her. Perhaps it would be wise to speak of what had happened, and see if there was a way for them to proceed from where they had left off last Season.

She shivered at the idea of opening her heart again. Stiffening her shoulders, she turned to him to reject his request. His eyes were hopeful, and at the same time uneasy. "Yes, that would be acceptable."

Lady Colborne led them from the dining room, the ladies chatting as they walked along. Marigold caught up to her and took her arm. "You and Lord Hertford seemed to be getting on much better."

"Hm." She wasn't about to commit herself, either to her sister, or in her own mind. She wanted to see where this walk led them before she made a final decision about him and their relationship. "Yes. It was a pleasant dinner."

The women scattered around the room, drinking tea, and conversing. Only about a half hour had passed when, as Juliet stood with Marigold and Charlotte exchanging wardrobe ideas, the gentlemen joined the ladies.

Graham broke free of the group of men as they entered the room and walked in her direction, his gaze never leaving hers. He advanced toward her like a sleek jungle animal on the prowl, his eyes dark and heavy-lidded, his movements graceful and smooth. Her breath caught, and a shiver ran down her arms. Heat pooled in the area between her legs, and her nipples tightened under her gown.

He nodded to the two ladies standing with her, and then with a slow, knowing smile, extended his hand. "A walk in the garden, my lady?"

Not even excusing herself from Charlotte and Marigold, she took his hand. Falling under his spell, and knowing this might not be her best decision, she walked with him through the opened French doors, into the cool night air, and the darkened garden.

CHAPTER EIGHT

Graham had fully expected to have Juliet refuse his hand when he walked up to her, despite her consent earlier at dinner. Now that he had her alone and in private, there was so much to say, he didn't know where to start.

Once they moved far enough away from the doors to be observed, he decided the best way to start the conversation was not with words. He swept her around, and taking her head in his hands, lowered his mouth to hers. His insides exploded with need as he met with her lips, moist, warm, and inviting. She opened, and he swooped in, tangling with her tongue, performing a dance that would lead them where his body desperately wanted to go. Her body seemed to agree as she sagged, and her hands moved up to grip his arms.

"Lady Juliet?" The soft feminine voice rang out in the night air, causing them to split apart, panting heavily, staring at each other.

Juliet took in a deep breath. "Yes, Lady Crampton. I'm over here." She began to move, but he took her arm and they strolled back toward the patio together.

"Fix the sides of your hair," he mumbled under his breath.

Juliet released her hand, and patted her hair, then took his arm once more.

Lady Crampton stood on the top step of the patio. "I don't think it is wise to be out here alone, my dear." She cast a look at Graham. "I'm sure you understand, my lord. It would not do to have Lady Juliet's reputation called into question."

He offered her a stiff bow. "You are absolutely correct, madam. I apologize for my thoughtlessness. May we have your permission to remain on the patio, in view of the room?"

"Is that what you wish, Juliet?"

"Yes, please. Just for a few moments. It was quite warm in the drawing room."

Lady Crampton dipped her head. "I shall expect you inside shortly." With a final warning glance at Graham, she turned and glided through the French doors.

He grinned at her. "I'm afraid I am not used to you having such a stalwart chaperone."

"Yes, Papa felt he wasn't doing a good enough job of guarding his daughters' reputations."

Graham had heard rumors that Juliet's sister and her husband, Lord and Lady St George had welcomed their first born a mere six months after the wedding. That had been a matter he had never considered until he was well on his way to Paris with Amy. He could have left Juliet in the same condition. With her unable to contact him. Every time he thought about that, he felt as though a bucket of cold water had been tossed on him.

"Juliet, we need time together. Alone. I don't believe I have yet to convince you I am serious in my wish for us to marry. I do not consider you a woman of easy virtue, nor do I wish to have an affair with you. I want you for my marchioness. That had always been my plan."

"Yet, you still have not told me to where you hied off to last year without so much as a by-your-leave."

He took both of her hands in his, and kissed her knuckles as he gazed at her. "You must believe me that I am unable to tell you. It was a promise I made to someone who means a great deal to me. Please just believe it had nothing to do with us, or my feelings for you."

"What are your feelings for me?"

The moment had arrived. He'd known for some time that he was hopelessly in love with Juliet. He wanted nothing more than her by his side for the rest of his life. A life he would find desolate without her in it.

Still haunted by her possible rejection, nevertheless, he took her by the shoulders. "I am in love with you. So desperately in love that I am a candidate for besotted gentleman of the year. I want you for my wife, the mother of our children. One word from you, and I will visit with your father and sign the marriage contracts."

She studied him for a full minute, apparently trying to see what was in his eyes. Which at this point was his heart.

"Lady Juliet, Lord Hertford, I believe the games are beginning and I know you don't want to miss out." Lady Crampton stood at the door, apparently not budging from her spot until her charge returned to the drawing room. Virtue and reputation intact.

Graham took Juliet's elbow and leaned close to her ear. "There is a picnic tomorrow. Tell Lady Crampton you cannot attend because you are suffering from a megrim."

She glanced at him but didn't answer. It was the last time he could speak with her for the rest of the night.

***

The next afternoon, Graham joined the rest of the party at the front of the house, awaiting the carriages and wagons that would transport them all to the picnic area Lady Colborne had selected.

He remained intent on the gathering of guests, hoping Juliet had, indeed, stayed behind with complaints of a megrim. Whether she did or did not, he would travel with the group to the picnic area to keep Lady Crampton from suspicion. Once the activities had begun, he would slip away and join her in her room.

Unless she had decided against his plan.

He held his breath when Lady Crampton and Lady Marigold walked through the front door to join the picnickers. He watched the door to see if Juliet would join them. When the crowed began to move forward, chatting away and arms linked, Lady Crampton and Lady Marigold moved with them, with no indication they were waiting for Juliet.

He breathed a sigh of relief.

***

Juliet paced in her room, calling herself any number of foolish names. She must have been out of her mind to agree to Graham's plan. Not only had she lied to Lady Crampton, who was fast becoming a treasured friend, she was leaving herself open to ruination if anyone got wind of his plan.

More than once she reached for her shawl and bonnet as she watched the picnickers climb into the vehicles headed to the picnic area. Then, remembering what she and Graham had shared before, she dropped the articles on the bed and continued her pacing.

For over an hour after the last carriage left, she vacillated between terror and excitement. She attempted to read, but threw the book down after reading the same page four times. She paced. She tried her hand at the embroidery piece she'd brought with her, but after tearing out fifteen minutes' worth of work, she cast that aside, also.

She was staring out the window when there was a light scratch at the door. She flew across the room and flung open the door. Graham leaned against the doorframe, his arms crossed, a rakish smirk on his lips. "I've come to soothe your megrim."

Reaching out, she yanked him into the room. "Are you crazy? There are servants up and down these halls all the time."

He took her in his arms. "They are paid to remain silent."

Juliet snorted, thinking of past employees of her father who had a penchant for gossip. Before she could dispute him, he tugged her close and cupped her cheeks. "I love you, Juliet. I know there is much more to be said between us, but you must believe me when I say that I cannot live the rest of my life without you."

She'd fought it as long as she could. Her eyes tearing, she said, "I love you, too. I tried so hard to hate you, forget you, ignore you, but it is not working." She pulled away and hugged herself. "But I am so afraid. I could never survive another broken heart."

"I would never intentionally do anything to hurt you. You must believe me." He reached out to her. She regarded accepting his hand as the final step in sealing the bond between them that had been broken. Slowly, she raised her hand and joined it with his. With a groan, he pulled her close, lifting her into his arms and laying her on the bed, coming down on top of her.

His lips were everywhere. On her cheeks, her eyelids, her mouth, jaw, and the soft skin under her ear. At the same time, her hands were frantically tugging on his cravat, flinging it to the floor and licking and sucking the skin at the base of his neck. Graham's hands reached behind her and his delft fingers undid her gown, then the ribbons of her stays.

Within minutes they were both naked, skin-to-skin, breathless and hearts pounding. "Oh, God, I dreamt of this for months." Graham smoothed the hair from her face. "You are so beautiful, and I adore you," he croaked.

Juliet was having a hard time holding back her tears. For so long she'd relegated their prior love making to the 'never again' part of her brain. She studied his mouth, his lips full and moist. "Show me."

He took her lips in a surprisingly gentle kiss, almost as if worshipping her mouth. Little nibbles, tender brushing with his tongue, and soft touches. As much as she enjoyed his tender ministrations, he left her mouth burning with fire. Taking things into her own hands, she kissed him with a hunger that shocked her.

Graham joined her fevered pitch, smothering her lips with demanding mastery. After marking her mouth as his, he moved down, his lips touching her nipple with tantalizing possessiveness. He nipped, then soothed the turgid peak. Juliet threw her head back when he suckled hard. "Yessssss."

She felt his lips widen to a grin as he placed kisses all over her body. She reached for his cock, and squeezed, eliciting a guttural groan. He moved his mouth down, forcing her to release him, stopping to encircle her belly button with his tongue, then continue until he reached the curls at the juncture of her thighs, already moistened from is kisses. He spread her legs and hooked them over his shoulders. She'd never felt so open, so exposed in her life. Yet, the desire to have him continue compelled her beyond all reason.

The first lick had her moaning, the second, third and fourth brought a rush of pleasure she'd remembered from their last coupling. Her breath caught and every color she'd ever seen flashed in her mind as she twisted and gripped the bed covers, and bit her lips to keep from crying out.

"Ah, sweetheart, I love the expression on your face when you reach pleasure. But this will not be the only time. We have a few hours before the others will return. I intend to produce that look many times." He dropped her legs and crawled up her body, resting comfortably between her legs.

Still not having recovered, she wrapped her arms around his neck, pulling him close. "That was wonderful," she gasped. He lowered his head and kissed her. She tasted herself on his lips, musky, sensual, and oh, so naughty. Just like his tongue.

His manhood pushed against her side, hard and pulsing. She covered it with her hand and Graham sucked in air through his teeth. "What say you we get on with it before I disgrace myself, and we have a repeat performance or two so we can take our time?" He rose on his elbows and studied her. "I'm afraid I have been far too anxious to bed you to last very long this first time."

***

Her answer was a deep kiss as her hips rose to meet his. Taking her movements as consent, Graham placed his cock at her entrance, and slowly slid in, both holding their breath at the wonderful sensation of their joining.

He rested his head in the crook of her neck, as feelings of love, possession, and homecoming swept over him. This was what he'd waited for all his life. This feeling of completion that only Juliet could bring him. No matter how many women he'd bedded, he'd never felt this way before. He wanted her, and only her.

He set the rhythm that would transport them both to a magical place where only lovers dwelt. The place where he and Juliet were bound, where they gave everything of themselves to each other.

Holding nothing back.

Graham covered Juliet's mouth with a soul-crushing kiss to block her scream as he poured his life force into her. With a shattering finish, he collapsed onto her, then quickly rolled and pulled her against his side. Their arms wrapped around each other, they lay panting, the air filled with the scent of their coupling, of the sound of their heartbeats, and the whoosh of their lungs gasping for air.

***

A few days later, the house guests all gathered in the ballroom for the final night of the house party. Gentry from the adjoining village had been invited as well. The dinner preceding the ball had been noteworthy, the food superb, and the wine excellent. Graham's only complaint was not having Juliet next to him for the meal. Their hostess had properly rearranged seating for each dinner so all the guests could interact with each other.

Graham was frustrated at the lack of opportunity he had to be alone with Juliet after their rousing bouts of love making the afternoon of the picnic. He was anxious for the party to end so he could visit with her father, state his intentions, and work out the marriage contracts.

Followed by a short betrothal.

He had been concerned the night following the picnic when Lady Crampton made a point of mentioning how she missed him, with all the guests and activities that afternoon. The look in her eye told him she had strong suspicions his disappearance had a lot to do with Juliet's megrim.

Which was probably why he and Juliet had not been left unchaperoned for the rest of the party. Lady Crampton and Juliet had been joined at the hip for the remainder of the time. He would not be surprised to learn the companion had taken to sleeping in front of Juliet's bedchamber door each night.

As much as he would have liked a repeat performance of that afternoon, he soothed his continuous raging erection with the thought of soon having Juliet in his bed every night for the rest of his life.

He hoped when they got down to actual negotiations, she would permit a quick wedding. Generally, such a happening was viewed by the *ton* as a necessity to save the girl's reputation. He and Juliet might have a few raised brows cast in their direction, but he knew from Lord and Lady St. George's new babe arriving early that gossipers soon turned their attention and condemnation to other nefarious matters.

Graham waited at the entrance to the ballroom, sipping a glass of champagne, and swapping stories with Lord Applebaum and Mr. Demming. He nodded politely and offered a comment when necessary, but his attention was riveted on the door, waiting for Juliet to appear.

After what seemed like hours, Lady Crampton, Lady Marigold, and Juliet appeared at the entrance to the ballroom. Graham sucked in a breath and was completely mesmerized. Juliet wore a simple gown of lilac, with a silver transparent overlay. Her shiny, thick hair had been pulled back into a loose topknot, with delicate curls dangling at the side of her lovely face. Tiny earbobs swayed as she walked toward him, a gold locket resting on the creamy mounts of her luscious breasts. Precisely where he wanted to place his lips.

Time.

"Hertford?" Demming nearly shouted in his ear.

He turned. "What?"

"What? I've asked you the same question three times." He glanced in the direction Graham studied, and chuckled. "Ah, so it seems our friend here is about to step into the parson's mousetrap. My sympathy, old boy."

"Sod off, Demming." Graham shot him a churlish look and left the two men standing there with smirks on their idiot faces. He joined Juliet as the three women stopped to chat with several of the female guests.

He walked up behind her and grasped her elbow. Juliet turned toward him, and broke into a smile that warmed his insides, and he swore brought sunshine into the candlelit room.

He bowed over her hand. "Good evening, Lady Juliet."

God, how he loved addressing her so formally when he had memories of holding her naked and panting in his arms as she broke apart, calling his name. It was enough to bring his cock to a military salute. Something he would have to suppress, and soon, if he were to remain in the ballroom.

"May I request a dance?"

She viewed him with a slight smile, and humor in her eyes. "I will see if I have room, my lord."

He leaned in. "You better have lots of room, darling."

"Shh." She glanced sideways at Lady Crampton who was in the middle of a conversation with their hostess and didn't seem to have heard him. In any event, he did need to take care until he'd spoken with her father, signed the contracts, and the betrothal officially announced. It couldn't be soon enough for him.

The orchestra started up a waltz, and he extended his elbow, his brows raised. "My lady?" Juliet rested her fingers on his arm and they made their way to the dance area.

Holding her in his arms was wonderful and torture. He wanted them away from the crowd, alone, in bed, naked. He had to tamp down his lust or he would disgrace himself.

They waltzed, dipping and moving around the room, chatting amiably. The candlelight highlighted the blonde in her hair, and cast her complexion into a golden glow. He was mesmerized, and sure she would keep him that way for the rest of his life.

The music stopped, and he escorted her to the refreshment table. He'd only taken a sip of champagne when he was approached by a footman. "My lord, this message just arrived for you." The man held out a cream-colored vellum with the Duke of Reading's crest on it.

"Thank you," he nodded at the man. He opened the missive and his stomach muscles tightened.

My Lord Marquess,

Please return to London forthwith. The Duke of Reading has passed, and per the late duke's wishes, your presence is required.

Elijah Reynolds, Esq.
Solicitor to His Grace the Duke of Reading

CHAPTER NINE

Juliet grabbed Graham's arm. "What is it?" He'd turned quite pale, and his lips had tightened.

"I believe I once told you the Duke of Reading acted a guardian for me after my parents passed?"

"Yes." She'd remembered hearing about that time in his life, when darkness seemed to overcome him, and how the duke had saved him by not only acting as guardian, but keeping him at his estate instead of sending him to school where a great deal of bullying took place.

"Isn't there a daughter, also?"

"Yes. Amy. She will be devastated." He ran his fingers through his hair. "The duke suffered apoplexy a few weeks ago. This note informs me of his passing."

Juliet sucked in a breath. "Oh, Graham, I am so sorry. I know you were very fond of him, and he influenced your life a great deal."

He tapped the note against his chin. "I will need to see to his body being moved from London to his estate for the funeral."

Now it was Juliet's turn for distress. Was this another excuse he was using to abandon her?

Graham studied her, then took her by the elbow. "Come with me."

Lady Crampton immediately ceased her conversation. "Where are you taking Lady Juliet?" It was obvious from her demeanor that she had no intention of allowing them to wander off again.

"My lady, may request you join us somewhere quiet? There is something I must discuss with Lady Juliet, and I have no desire to cause any problems with her reputation."

His words seeming to ease her mind, Lady Crampton dipped her head and addressed Lady Colbourne. "I will return shortly. Please see that Lady Marigold enjoys herself."

Juliet smiled to herself. Lady Crampton's words meant, *keep an eye on this one, while I supervise that one.*

The three of them departed the ballroom and made their way down the corridor to the drawing room. She and Graham moved to the settee near the window, where pale moonlight shone through, while Lady Crampton discretely took a seat on the settee close to the door.

Graham wasted no time. "I see trepidation in your eyes."

Juliet raised her chin. "I have no idea to what you are referring, my lord."

"Don't do this, sweetheart. I see in your eyes

that you believe I will once again disappear, not to be heard from again."

Of course I think that. When will I ever learn?

"I think no such thing." She was certain the sound of her pounding heart—her soon to be broken heart—could stretch across the room to each Lady Crampton's ears.

He grinned. "Liar." He took both of her hands in his. "I will leave now and travel back to London to see to matters there. However, I will present myself to your father as early as possible tomorrow. What time would he receive me?"

She waited for a moment. Was it possible he was serious? That he was not using the unfortunate death of the duke as an excuse to once again leave her? She had to admit the past few weeks he had behaved in a truly gentlemanly manner. He'd not pushed her, or in any way behaved as the rake she'd thought him to be last Season.

"Papa generally retires to his study for a few hours every morning. Most days he is busy at his work by ten o'clock."

"I will be there. What time are you departing in the morning?"

Juliet pulled her hands from his and walked to where Lady Crampton sat. "When have you planned for us to leave?"

She granted Juliet a warm smile. "I had hoped to be on the road no later than eight o'clock. Will that suffice?"

"Yes. Thank you for your patience." Papa had truly found a jewel when he'd hired Lady Crampton.

She patted her hand. "Please, just finish up your conversation. Even with me here with you, we don't want to be absent for too long."

Graham watched her as she crossed back over to him. "Have I told you how lovely you look this evening? I had hoped to admire you for several more hours. And at least one more dance."

Still not sure where she stood with Graham, she merely dipped her head. "We will be leaving about eight o'clock."

"Then I will have already visited with your father by the time you return."

We will see.

"Now I must wish you good evening, and safe travels. I will return on my horse, Demon, and send Carson home in the carriage with my luggage." He squeezed her hands. "I cannot even kiss you goodbye."

"No. I am afraid not."

Instead, he raised her hand and kissed the sensitive skin on the back of her wrist at the opening of her glove. "Once I have visited with your father, I will be taken up with my duties to the duke's estate. I hope to be back in London within a week or two, depending on how extensive my immediate responsibilities are."

Her mouth dry, she merely nodded. He took

her by the elbow and walked her to Lady Crampton. "My lady, I bid you a good evening. I have been called to London and must depart immediately."

Lady Crampton stood and took Juliet's arm. "I wish you a safe journey, my lord."

With one final glance at Juliet, he dipped his head and left the room.

***

Graham stared at the swath of black material draped over the front door of the duke's London residence. He'd arrived home in the wee hours of the morning, grabbed a few hours of sleep, and then a quick bath and breakfast before heading here.

Taking a deep breath, he ascended the stairs just as the front door opened. The butler bowed. "Good morning, my lord."

"Good morning, Jason. Is the family about?"

"Her Grace arrived last evening and is still abed. Lady Amy is in the breakfast room."

"Thank you." He handed his hat, gloves and cane to the butler and continued onto the breakfast room. Amy sat at the table, a cup of tea in front of her. She looked up as he entered and burst into tears.

He held out his arms and she jumped from her seat and ran to him. "Papa is dead."

"I know, poppet. I am so sorry." He held her while she cried, rubbing her back and murmuring words of comfort. After a few minutes, he withdrew a handkerchief and handed it to her. She took it, and wiped her face.

"Have you had breakfast?" He smiled. Despite her distraught state, she remembered her manners.

Even though she was an adult, and older than him by two years, Graham had been named by the duke as her guardian. He'd already known from conversations with the duke once Graham had reach his majority, that the duke was appointing him guardian since he did not trust his wife to look out for Amy's best interests. He'd had the documents drawn up, and signed a few years ago. He'd also placed a considerable amount of money in trust for Amy, with only Graham having say over any disbursements. It seemed he *truly* did not trust the duchess.

"Yes. I have eaten, but I would love some tea." With his arm around her slight shoulders, he walked her back to the table and pulled out her chair. He took the seat across from her, and reached for her hand. "How are you doing?"

"Mama came last night. She's still upstairs." Amy twisted her fingers, always nervous around the duchess. The woman's displeasure in her only child was not well hidden. It was truly a pity the girl had been left with no family. Even if Amy was unable to move about in Society, it would not hurt the girl's mother to take more if an interest in her.

Amy was a charming girl, and could be quite

bright at times. There was nothing seriously wrong with her, except she was a bit slow. She certainly was pretty enough, had a beautiful smile, and a keen sense of humor.

"Graham, I want to ask you something." She pulled her brows together, and hesitated.

He gave her a warm smile. Amy was truly one of his favorite people. "What is it, poppet?"

"Do I have a lot of money now?"

He was taken aback, but then one never knew where Amy's mind was at any given moment. "You have sufficient money to last you for the rest of your life." He winked at her. "Unless you suddenly decide to take up gambling, or some other inappropriate undertaking."

She sat up straighter. "You are my guardian, correct?"

"Yessss." He dragged out the word. What was going on in her head? "Why do you ask?"

"Do I have enough money to buy a house? A nice house. In the country?"

"Honey, I don't advise you to make any decisions just yet. Even though your father's estates have passed onto his heir, there is no hurry for you to move. No one would expect that of you."

She waved away his statement. "I don't care about all of that. What I want to know is will you buy me a house in the country?"

"I will do whatever it is you want, if I believe it's in your best interest. That is what a guardian does. If you want to live in the country, I will be more than happy to ask my man of business to begin a search for something suitable."

"And there is one more thing."

Uh, oh. He had a funny feeling he was not going to like this. "What is that, poppet?"

She leaned forward, a look of determination in her eyes he'd never seen before. "I want to get married and return to Paris and get my baby."

***

Still musing on that strange conversation, Graham rode his horse into the mews behind Juliet's house and left Demon with the stable master. He'd ended up spending a couple of hours with Amy, and then more time than he wanted holding the duchess's hand while she tried to make him feel sorry for her because she'd lost the husband she'd never cared a whit about.

She also questioned him about money, and he had been delighted to tell she'd been left with more than enough funds to live a life of luxury. That seemed to brighten her sorrow at the passing of her husband.

The duchess had also made it quite clear she had no intention of involving her daughter in her life, and wished her well as she sailed out the front door, late for an appointment with her *modiste*. She'd told Graham she would travel to the estate to greet the mourners, and then head to the continent to "recover from my loss."

He shook his head. It was so sad the duke

had such a cold marriage. As he climbed the steps to Juliet's home, he thought on how he would have so much more in his marriage. He loved Juliet, and she loved him.

"Good morning, my lord."

"Good morning," he greeted Mason. "I sent around a note earlier requesting an audience with Lord Pomeroy. Is he available?"

"Yes. You are expected. If you will follow me to the library."

Lord Pomeroy hopped up when Graham entered the room. He strode across the space, his hand held out. No doubt the man guess why he was here, and was more than joyful to sign marriage contracts for yet another daughter.

"Hertford. Good to see you, son." Pomeroy waved him to a seat by the fireplace, taking the one across from him. "I've sent for coffee. As much as I enjoy a good cup of English tea, this time of the morning, I love a cup of coffee."

They chatted about the usual conversational openings until they each held a cup of coffee and a plate of delicate little sandwiches he remembered from his prior visit.

"So, what brings you around this morning, Hertford?"

He laid his plate down on the table and cleared his throat. "Sir. I am quite fond of Lady Juliet."

"Yes, yes. I suspected as much. Go on." He popped three of the sandwiches into his mouth at once. It was a shame the poor man couldn't get a decent sandwich in his own home.

"I have every reason to believe Lady Juliet is amenable to me asking you for permission to marry her."

"Wonderful. Congratulations." He beamed at him.

Graham couldn't help his eyebrows rising. "I take it that means you approve?"

Taking a sip of his coffee, he placed the cup on the table in front of them. "My boy, I love my daughters with my whole heart. They are the light of my life, and I would lay down my life for any one of them." His smile disappeared and he appeared more somber than he'd ever seen him. "I don't mind telling you when my wife passed on years ago, I was devastated." He made the sign of the cross, something that always amused him since the man was not Catholic.

"There was a time there, when I thought I would wallow in darkness for the rest of my life. Then my eldest, Elise, came to me one day in tears. She'd been mother to my other girls, and a problem had arisen with Marigold that she felt was beyond her capabilities." He winced. "Elise was all of ten years.

"It was then I realized although my beloved wife had left me, I still had three wonderful, beautiful reminders of our love."

His normally bright smile returned. "From that day on, I decided to be the best father ever."

He popped another sandwich into his mouth, chewed and swallowed. "Last year it came to me in a dream that I needed to share the joy, and make three men—unknown to me at the time— the happiest of men in England. By marrying my daughters."

Graham was having a hard time keeping the laughter inside. The man was certainly amusing.

"So to answer you, my boy, I am delighted that you have found the treasure in Juliet that I've always known was there."

Frowning at the table in front of them, he looked up. "What do you say we go to my club and get some decent food? We can work out the marriage contracts there." Pomeroy hopped up and strode to the door. Graham had to hurry to keep up with him. He grinned as his future father-in-law shouted to the man at the door to get his carriage brought around. He was certainly an energetic individual. And quite entertaining.

***

Juliet had been home from the house party for a few hours. Mason had offered the information that Lord Hertford had sent a missive around earlier that morning, had arrived for a meeting with Papa, and then the two of them had gone out to visit White's.

Her nerves had settled a bit at that news. At least Graham had kept his word about visiting with Papa, and since she had pried the information out of Mason that they had both seemed quite cheerful when they left, she assumed all was well with Graham's request for her hand.

She spent the afternoon helping Charlene wade through the gowns in her wardrobe to pack away those she no longer wore. If she was to be a married lady soon—butterflies danced in her stomach at that thought—she would require a whole new wardrobe to suit her new station in life.

The Marchioness of Hertford.

She giggled like a schoolgirl, and chastised herself for her foolishness. She was reading a book in her sitting room when the sound of carriage wheels drew her attention to the window.

The Pomeroy carriage drew up, and both Papa and Graham alighted. They laughed and chatted quite loudly as they approached the door. Papa had his arm flung about Graham's shoulders, and it looked from where she stood that they both had had a bit to drink.

Within minutes there was a scratch at her door. Mason stood there, looking a bit discombobulated. "My lady, his lordship requests your presence in the library." His usual somber demeanor was missing, and he looked as if he had no idea what to do next.

"Thank you. I will be down momentarily."

"Ah, my lady. . ."

"Yes?"

"His lordship requests you bring Lady

Crampton and Lady Marigold with you."

She frowned. Odd, that. She had assumed Papa was going to talk to her about the wedding plans, and perhaps include Graham in some of the conversation. But for the life of her, she couldn't understand why Lady Crampton and Marigold had to be there.

"Fine. I will bring them with me."

She hurried to her dressing table and quickly fixed her hair as best she could and then tapped on both Lady Crampton and Marigold's doors. Unable to explain to them what Papa wanted, the three women descended the stairs and marched to the library. Both Papa and Graham were waving their hands in conversation, and laughing quite loudly.

Papa noticed them and waved them in. "Ah, here they are. Such lovely women I am lucky to lay eyes on every day."

Juliet stared at Marigold with raised brows, and poor Lady Crampton blushed to the roots of her hair. "Papa, you wanted to see us?"

'Yes, yes. Come in, don't hover in the doorway." He waved them to the settee near the fireplace. "Your young man here wants to say something to you."

Juliet was horrified. Surely Graham did not plan to propose to her right here in front of all these people? She gasped and looked at him. He seemed to be having some trouble standing, and leaned quite heavily on the back of a chair, as he gave her a very suspicious grin.

Good God, they were both in their cups! And it was barely five in the afternoon.

"Papa, I think perhaps it might be wise to postpone whatever it is that Lord Hertford plans to say until another time."

"No. There is no time like the present, young lady." He hiccupped.

"Papa, I don't think it's necessary for everyone to be here." She was never so humiliated in her life. Here she was about to receive a proposal from the man she loved, who was so foxed he could barely stand up, in front of her entire family.

He waved, and stumbled a bit himself. "Nonsense. Don't you remember how we were all there when Lord St. George proposed to your sister? 'Twas lovely."

"Yes, I remember, but I had no idea it was to become a family tradition." Her sister had been so adamant she would not marry that her now husband had been forced to recite a love poem at one of Elise's gatherings to get her attention. And consent.

Lady Crampton cleared her throat. "My lord, I think perhaps it would be better if we all leave the room, and allow Lord Hertford and Lady Juliet some privacy."

"No. Not necessary." Graham attempted to straighten his cravat that looked as though it was strangling him. He walked, sort of sideways, over in her direction. "My love, I would like to speak to you."

Juliet didn't know whether to laugh or cry. Instead, she dropped her head into her hands and groaned. Lady Crampton walked up to her. "My dear, I think it would be better if you sat." She leaned in closer to whisper in her ear, "Then you will be able to catch his lordship if he tumbles over."

She raised her head and looked at her companion. "Is this really happening?"

Lady Crampton gave her a tight smile. "Yes, my dear, I am afraid it is. However, one must endeavor to make the best of every situation."

Papa smiled brightly at Lady Crampton. "By God, I believe I made an excellent choice when I hired you, madam."

She sighed deeply. "Please take a seat, my lord. You are above to fall over."

Papa sat, Graham fell to his knees, wincing, most likely because of the way he landed, while Lady Crampton and Marigold took the settee near the window. They all waited with bated breath.

"My love." Graham stopped and reached for her hand, which he missed and grabbed her knee to keep from falling sideways. "My love, I wish you would make me the happiest of men by becoming my march . . . marchon . . . marchioness." He beamed as though he were a lad reciting his alphabet for the first time.

"Oh, Graham. I had hoped to have a much

more romantic proposal."

He leaned forward, again leaning on her knees. "Shh. You should not call me Graham." He looked around the room as though it was populated with spies. "They will all guess . . . you know."

Oh, good Lord, if the floor did not open up and swallow her, she would expire from mortification right here on the spot. Her face aflame, she glanced sideways at Papa who continued to smile, so he either hadn't heard, or didn't understand. Marigold had the same look on her face, but Lady Crampton blinked several times and then her eyes widened, her lips pursed in speculation.

Before anyone could say anything, with a soft sigh, Graham fell flat on his face.

Papa hiccupped. "I think we should celebrate with a drink." He raised his voice. "Mason, bring the champagne."

***

The next afternoon, Juliet, Lady Crampton and Marigold visited the *modiste* to begin preparations for her new wardrobe and gowns for all of them to wear to the wedding. After the disastrous proposal the day before, Juliet had two footmen put Graham in one of the bedchambers to sleep off his over-indulgence.

She'd heard Lady Crampton and Papa exchanging heated words, but once she knew Graham was settled for the night, she ordered a hot bath, a tray in her room, and a sleeping draught.

Early this morning Graham had greeted her in the breakfast room with a rather sheepish expression. When he ascertained he had been forgiven for his rather inept proposal, he told her he would be leaving that afternoon to arrange for the duke's funeral, and removal of his body from London to the family estate where the burial would take place.

He held her in his arms and assured her he would be back in plenty of time for the wedding. "I can't wait to make you my wife. It will be hard being away from you for the next few weeks, but easier on my physical state with you not near." He grinned, kissed her once more and departed.

Papa, looking as sharp and fresh as any other morning, requested she attend him once she'd finished her breakfast. It was then that he told her the marriage contracts were all worked out, and signed. He also indicated Lady Crampton was insisting on a short betrothal, so the wedding was going forward.

As soon as the banns were called for three weeks, they would wed. He'd told her when he had resisted, insisting it was not enough time to put on a proper wedding, Lady Crampton had calmly assured him she had everything in hand, and all would be ready for the wedding in a month's time.

With it all moving so quickly, they needed to

see to her wardrobe. Although the proposal had been less than romantic, she was excited about the upcoming wedding. She loved Graham, and he loved her. They would have a wonderful life together.

CHAPTER TEN

Graham followed Amy and her companion, Miss Downing, into the Duke of Readings crested carriage. They were following the vehicle transporting the duke's body to his estate in Suffolk for burial. The duchess elected to travel in her own coach, stating she was too distraught to travel with the others. It had taken a lot of effort, but Graham managed not to laugh when she made that ridiculous statement. More than anything, it was Amy's sigh of relief at her mother's announcement that had him holding his tongue.

"Have you thought on my request, Graham?" Amy's big blue eyes did not hold the sparkle they ordinarily did.

"About the house in the country?"

"Yes. I want a house, and I want my baby."

He had given their conversation quite a bit of thought. He knew had His Grace not passed away, he would not have wanted his daughter to marry the man the duke was certain had taken advantage of her.

However, Graham was not entirely sure Amy

had been taken advantage of. She seemed to sincerely love this man—whoever he was, she would not say—and unless she was over estimating the man's feelings, he loved her as well.

Graham reached over and patted her hand. "Let us get through the funeral before we tackle that problem."

"Do you promise?" Her tear-filled eyes twisted his insides. As her appointed guardian, this was a decision he now had to make. Although he would consider the late duke's feelings on the matter were he alive, the fact was His Grace was not alive. Amy was, and Graham would find it exceedingly hard to deny her something she wanted so badly.

The rest of the trip was taken up by Miss Downing reading aloud to the three of them, and Amy taking a nap. Graham watched her while she slept. She was a beautiful girl—woman actually, although it was hard for him to think of her that way. It was truly not difficult to believe this man who had fathered her baby loved her. For her sake, he hoped when he met with him, her lover was not a manipulative man who was only interested in Amy's money.

That would break her heart. And his would take a beating, also.

They were settled at Reading Hall for a few hours when the duchess arrived. She was younger than the duke by twelve years. Although not such an unusual occurrence in their class, the age difference might have accounted for the poor relations they had with each other. At seven and forty years, she had kept herself looking quite young. Not pretty in the classic way, she had an air of sophistication about her that attracted many men. From what Graham had heard, she certainly had no problem keeping her bed warm while living separate from the duke.

There were times when Graham had often thought one of the reason the duchess had so little to do with Amy was a bit of jealousy of the girl's beauty. As horrible as it sounded, the duchess might not have been sorry that her daughter was kept away from the *ton*, and therefore no competition for her mother.

"I need a bath sent up and a tray in my room." She patted Amy on the head as she passed, like she was some type of household pet. Graham had to hold his tongue, lest he start trouble. As annoyed as he was, a funeral was not the time or place to chastise the woman. Not that it would make a difference, anyway.

Three days followed of mourners coming to the house, listening to Her Grace wax eloquently on how much the duke would be missed, what a wonderful man he'd been, an outstanding husband, and devoted father.

Amy hid most of the time, and Graham smiled a lot more than he wanted to. When the final coach carrying the last of the mourners pulled away from the Hall, Graham breathed a sigh of relief. Her Grace departed soon after, with smiles, pats, and the scent of expensive perfume.

Not once had she asked Graham what arrangements had been made for her daughter.

He shook his head as her carriage drove away, reminding himself he needed to get back to London and make the final preparations for his wedding, with was now a little more than a week away.

It had been decided that Amy and Miss Downing would remain at the Hall until other arrangements could be made for them. Amy still insisted she wanted Graham to buy her a house.

Later that afternoon, Graham sat at the duke's large desk in the library, going over last minute papers that needed his signature before he departed early the next morning. A scratch at the door drew his attention. "Enter."

Amy stuck her head in. "May I have a moment, Graham?"

He smiled and leaned back, his arms resting on the chair. "Of course, Amy. Any time."

The door opened wider and Amy entered, with a gentleman following her. Graham's muscles tightened and he went on alert. No doubt, this was the man who'd fathered Amy's baby.

The man appeared to be in his late thirties. He was dressed as a gentleman, and held himself in a dignified manner. He neither bowed and scraped, nor gave Graham an arrogant look. He appeared to be a pleasant man, with enough wrinkles alongside his mouth to tell he smiled quite a bit.

"Graham, I would like you to meet Mr. Francis Boyle." He drew him forward, and said, "Francis, this is my guardian, and very close friend, the Marquess of Hertford."

Both men studied each other, neither smiling, neither backing down. Mr. Boyle bowed, low enough to show respect, but not subservience. "My lord."

Stunned at this turn of events, he waved at the chairs in front of the massive desk. "Please, have a seat."

They did not release hands as they sat side by side. Amy glowed with happiness, and yes, he had to admit, with love. Mr. Boyle was more reserved, but in his position, Graham would have been the same.

The awkward silence was thankfully interrupted by Amy. "Graham, Mr. Boyle has something to say to you." She nodded in his direction. The look the man gave Amy had Graham straightening in his chair. No one could fake that type of adoration unless he were treading the boards at Drury Lane.

Boyle cleared his throat. "My lord, I am here to formally request permission from you, as Amy's guardian, to marry her. Frankly, I do not understand why she needs a guardian at her age, but since that is the situation, I shall deal with it."

Well, then.

Graham drew his attention away from the man. "Amy, I would prefer Mr. Boyle and I speak in private."

A look of alarm crossed her face, but Boyle patted her hand. "It's all right, love. You go on and have yourself some tea. I will join you shortly. These things are better handled between men."

Graham had to bite back a chuckle as Amy glanced between him and her young man— although in retrospect, he was probably a good ten years older than Graham—and chewed her lip. Although a bit slow in most matters, Amy had a streak of independence that always amused Graham. She studied the two men.

Boyle stood and raised Amy with him. "'Tis fine, Amy. Do not worry yourself, 'tis not good for your health."

She nodded and left the room. Boyle sat back down and the two eyed each other once again. "So you want to marry Amy."

Boyle nodded. "Yes, sir. We have loved each other for more than two years now. I begged her to allow me to speak with His Grace while he was alive, but she said she wished to approach him first. When she did, and told him she was in a family way. I did not see her until two days ago when she returned here for her father's funeral. I have been sick with worry about her, and sent numerous letters to her in London.

"I also traveled to London twice, and was barred from the duke's home by a very stodgy butler. All he would tell me was Amy was on the continent on holiday. It wasn't until she returned that I learned what had happened to our baby." His fists tightened on the arm of the chair. "I want to marry her, and bring our child home, and provide for my family. She is devastated at what her father did to her."

"You do know Amy is quite wealthy?" It was time to hold Boyle to the fire. So far Graham was impressed with the man, but as her guardian he had to look out for her best interests.

Boyle waved his hand in dismissal. "Perhaps. That is not my concern. I own a spacious cottage, with an extensive farm that provides a tidy income. In addition, I acquired a bookstore in the village that was left to me by my father. I have more than sufficient income to provide for my family."

"Are you aware that Amy wants me to buy a house for her? I am assuming she means for it to be for the two of you."

"I will speak with her about that. We will decide together. However, I do want to make myself clear on one point. Aside from purchasing a house, if that is what she wants, the rest of her money will be put into a trust for our children. I do not need, nor want, her money."

More impressed by the minute, he had to

tackle two more issues. "Amy is the daughter of a duke. She has been raised with every luxury that money can buy. Do you think it fair of you to ask her to live such a different life?"

Boyle hopped up and leaned over, his hands flattened on the desk. "I am fully aware of the differences in our stations. However, from what I've seen and heard of her family so far, all they've done is hide her away. She is a beautiful, loving, funny woman. I love her, and will treat her like a queen, even if I cannot afford to provide all the luxuries she's had all her life.'"

He moved back, and tugged on his jacket sleeves. "You said there were two issues?"

Still reeling from Boyle's near explosion, Graham had to think for a minute. "Yes. You are aware, I am sure, that one of the reasons Amy was, as you put it, 'hidden away,' was because she is what Society deems a bit slow." He hated saying that, but he had to get it all out there.

Boyle snorted. "I care nothing for what Society believes. What is important to me is I love her, and want to take care of her for the rest of our lives. She desperately wants our baby back. I agree, and we will take the trip to Paris to retrieve the child. I hope to do all of this as a married couple, and with your permission."

Graham remained silent for a few minutes, thinking over what they'd just discussed. "I will admit I am quite impressed with you, Boyle. I love Amy like a sister, and only want to do what is best for her. I also want her to be happy."

He stood, indicating the interview was over. "However, I am needed in London for my own wedding. I promise I will give careful consideration to your request, and will return with my wife to discuss this further."

Boyle gave him a wiry smile. "Please do not put this aside for too long, my lord. Amy is quite distressed, and I will not allow her pain to continue indefinitely." With those parting words, he bowed, and left the room.

Graham sat and shifted in the chair to look out the window. If Mr. Francis Boyle turned out to be true to his word, this would be the best thing in the world for Amy. A normal life, a loving husband who sees no deficiency, and a family. But, on the side of caution, he would hire a Bow Street runner to investigate the man before he made his decision.

***

Lord Comerford returned Juliet from their dance to Lady Crampton's side. "Is something wrong?" Juliet eyed her chaperone with concern. Lady Crampton was pale as new snow, and she gripped her hands together. "I believe we should depart for home."

"Whatever is the matter? Are you ill?"

"No. I need to speak with you, and we must head for home."

Confused, and somewhat concerned, given her chaperone's normally well-composed demeanor, she nodded. "Yes, of course. If that is what you wish. What about Marigold?"

"Oh, dear. I forgot about her."

Forgot about her? Something was dreadfully wrong for Lady Crampton to forget one of her charges. "Shall I find her?"

"Yes. Please do. I will meet you at the entrance hall and request our carriage be brought around." With those departing words, she hurried away, scooting around clusters of guests, nodding briefly, but continuing on her way when two women attempted to stop her.

Shaking her head, Juliet made her rounds of the various groups conversing between dances until she spotted her sister in a group of young ladies and gentlemen. Juliet waved to gain her attention.

Once they were on their way to the entrance hall, Marigold tugged on Juliet's hand. "Whatever is going on?"

Juliet didn't know why, but for some reason her heart was pounding and her mouth had tried up. The anxiety and concern on Lady Crampton's face scared her. Hopefully she hadn't received word that something had happened to Papa. Or Elise's baby!

Completely tied in knots by the time they joined Lady Crampton, and they all three settled into the carriage, Juliet said, "What has happened? You are frightening me."

"I am so sorry, Juliet, but I must ask you to

wait until we have arrived home. I wish for your father to be present."

Blowing out a deep breath, Juliet collapsed back on her seat. Well, nothing then was the matter with Papa, and if it were Elise's babe, it was highly unlikely Lady Crampton would have found this out at the Livingston's ball.

The three women remained silent until the carriage drew up to the townhouse. Juliet's nerves were stretched as thin as springtime ice on a pond. At any moment, she felt as though she would shatter, and had no reason to think why, only that she knew for some reason whatever was troubling her companion had to do with her.

Once then entered the house and handed over their pelisses, bonnets and reticules to the butler, Mrs. Crampton turned to Marigold. "My dear, will you please ask your father to join your sister and I in the drawing room? I'm afraid I must ask you to wait in your bedchamber until we are finished."

Oh, good heavens, this got worse by the minute.

Juliet paced from wall to wall in the drawing room as they waited for Papa. Lady Crampton had regained her composure and was sitting on the settee near the fireplace, her hands crossed daintily on her lap.

"What's all this about?" Papa entered the room, his booming voice making both Lady Crampton and Juliet jump. He peered at Lady

Crampton over the tops of his spectacles low on his nose. "Marigold rushed into my library, all atwitter that I should join the two of you here in the drawing room. I expected to see swooning or at least a bit of blood, given Marigold's distraction."

"I am so sorry for the upset, my lord." Lady Crampton looked up at Papa who loomed over her.

He glanced back and forth between the two women. "Brandy." Walking to the sideboard, he tossed over his shoulder, "Juliet, my dear, for heaven's sake take a seat. I have no idea what is going on, but wearing out the carpet will not make it better."

Her stiff legs carried her across the room and she sat next to Lady Crampton, who took her hand in hers Even through their gloves, she felt the coldness of her companion's hands.

Papa offered each of them a glass of brandy. Lady Crampton took a sip of hers, and waved to a chair for Papa to sit. Her companion was indeed beside herself, since she had just ordered her employer to sit down.

She placed her glass on the small table in front of them, and turned to Juliet. "At the Livingston ball this evening, I had a conversation with Lady Windham. It seems she and her husband just returned from holiday on the continent."

Papa leaned forward when Lady Crampton

reached for her glass and took a sip. "She told me last summer while they were on the packet headed to Calais, they met a young woman who they conversed with quite a bit. It seems the girl was in a family way, and off to stay with her aunt in Paris for the time of her confinement.

"The girl spoke of the child she carried, and how much she loved the babe's father. She said there were some complications, but she was sure they would marry. This shocked Lady Windham to some extent, since the girl spoke so openly about it, and she was obviously of the upper classes. She was a sweet girl, pretty, delicate, and Lady Windham thought, a little bit on the slow side, if you know what I mean."

The tightness in her belly growing with every moment, Juliet merely nodded.

Lady Crampton took a deep breath, and glanced at Papa. Her hands tightened on Juliet's. "I am so sorry to tell you this. You know how much I love you, and do not want to see you hurt."

Tears already filling her eyes, Juliet nodded once more, her stiff lips barely moving. "Go on."

"Lady Windham and her husband left the packet in Calais and saw the girl once more. She was walking away from the boat, and turned to wave goodbye to them. The man whose arm she clung to turned also."

She stopped and took a deep breath. "The man accompanying her was Lord Hertford."

CHAPTER ELEVEN

It was the third day since Juliet had cancelled her wedding. She'd spent the time in her room, first cutting into strips her wedding gown, and then feeding the pieces into the fireplace. She refused to leave her bedchamber, or accept company. Every tray of food that arrived was returned untouched.

She knew there would be complications, but she was sure they would marry.

It was interesting. Never in her life had Juliet been a *complication*. The darkness that had overcome her when she awoke from the swoon Lady Crampton's words had caused had not lifted for one single moment. She did not know what day it was, or if it was breakfast or dinner on the last tray she'd sent away.

She hadn't bathed, brushed her hair, or slept. One glance in the mirror told her how horrible she looked. Not that she cared. Moving to the bed, she sat at the edge and contemplated what disturbed her the most about her situation.

Like her sister before her, it seemed she too

was in a family way with no husband. And from what she'd heard, the man she'd expected to be that husband already had a child with another woman who was madly in love with him.

True, given the stress of the wedding plans, and Graham being away, her courses could merely be late. However, given she was as regular as clockwork, and she and Graham had sexual relations a few weeks ago, it did not bode well for her.

Of course, perhaps she, Graham, and the mother of his other child could travel together to a country where they allowed more than one wife, and all live together as one big happy family. She groaned at her own thoughts and crawled up on the bed, smothering her head in the pillow. Tears, that seemed to be a huge part of her life lately burst from her eyes, and she sobbed.

A scratch at the door had her wiping her eyes. "Yes?"

"Juliet, it's Marigold. Let me in."

She'd already turned Marigold away once, and Lady Crampton twice, but it seems they were not going to leave her alone, so she might as well endure this visit. Truth be known, she was quite tired of her own sad company,

"Enter."

Her sister poked her head around the door. "Are you all right?"

Juliet drew her knees up and wrapped her arms around her legs. "Why wouldn't I be all right? I just leaned my erstwhile betrothed accompanied his pregnant lover to France last year. Fool that I am, I allowed him to convince me the time away meant nothing to him, and accepted his proposal."

Marigold entered the room and sat alongside her on the bed.

Juliet rested her chin on her knees. "And now I have reason to believe Lord Hertford has another pregnant lover to deal with."

At first Marigold looked confused, then she sucked in a deep breath. "Oh no. Truly?"

She turned to rest her cheek on her knees, looking Marigold in the eye. "Do you think I would joke about something like that right now?"

***

It had taken Graham two days more after his meeting with Boyle to finish up what he needed to do in Suffolk. In the meantime, he sent a missive to his man of business in London to have him look into Boyle's background.

He was bone weary when he arrived at his London townhouse, having ridden through, only stopping for food and to change horses. Trudging up the stairs, he greeted his butler as the door swung open. The look on the man's face brought him up short. "What is wrong?"

"Good day, my lord. Lady Crampton has been for a visit twice. She left a note for you the last time, urging that I present it to you the minute you arrive."

"Lady Crampton? Lady Juliet's companion?"

"Yes, sir." He held out a piece of cream-colored vellum. "Here."

Frowning, and a bit concerned, he opened the missive.

My Lord Marquess,

It is of the upmost importance that you meet with me as quickly as possible. Please send a note upon your return. I will meet you at Gunter's at whatever time you state. Please do not call at Lord Pomeroy's townhouse.

Lady Selina Crampton

What the devil was going on? Had Juliet taken ill? He dashed off a note to Lady Crampton that he would meet her at Gunter's in an hour's time. That gave him enough time to bathe, and present himself as a gentleman.

Any fatigue he'd felt upon arriving home vanished at the note. He tapped the paper against his lips as he hurried upstairs after ordering a footman to have his bath prepared since Carson was behind him in a carriage with his luggage.

It was exactly an hour later that Graham arrived at Gunter's. Not seeing Lady Crampton immediately, he took a table and ordered tea and pastries. Within minutes, Lady Crampton hurried up to him. By the look on her face he had a feeling she had not arrived with good news.

Right now, only a few days before their wedding, Juliet's companion should have been very busy with fittings, floral arrangements and menu planning, not taking out time for surreptitious meetings with the intended groom. He stood as she arrived at the table. "My lady." He bowed and pulled out a chair for her.

Her face was flushed under the veiled hat she wore. She almost looked as if she were trying to disguise herself. Something was terribly wrong, and a very uncomfortable feeling caused knots to form in his stomach. "Tea, my lady?"

She seemed almost surprised to see the tea things on the table. She nodded and poured herself a cup and took a sip. Her hand shook as she placed the cup in the saucer.

"What is it, my lady?"

"A few nights ago, Lady Juliet, Lady Marigold and I attended a ball at Lord and Lady Livingston's house." She stopped and took another sip of tea. "While I was there, I had a conversation with Lady Windham. She told me the story of a trip she and her husband took last year to France."

Bloody hell. Did the woman see him and Amy? He broke into a sweat. "And what of it, madam?"

Lady Crampton leaned forward. "She saw you and a young lady leave the packet from Dover to Calais together. The young lady had befriended her during the journey and told a story of being with child, and very much in love with the babe's father. She was apparently being escorted to Paris to have the child there." She gave him a quelling look. "Away from the eyes of London."

He sucked in a deep breath, fighting the panic that started in his toes and raced all the way to his pounding heart. "And of course you told Lady Juliet?"

She stiffened in her seat and glared at him. "It was my duty, my lord. Well you should know Lady Juliet has cancelled the wedding, and will not speak to anyone the past three days. She won't eat, she doesn't sleep, and we are all worried sick over her." She placed her hands around the tea cup and raised her chin, the fire of a woman protecting her young in her eyes. "What have you to say for yourself, Lord Hertford?"

***

Lord Maxwell Pomeroy stood at the window to his library, his hands clasped behind his back. One of his little girls was heartbroken, and he wanted to take his fists to someone. Not to someone. To one particular one.

The Honorable, the Marquess of Hartford. He snorted. Nothing honorable about the man. Once the man showed himself in London, he would invite him to Gentleman Jim's and beat the living daylights out of him. No matter that he was a few years older, he was angry enough to do the scoundrel real damage. No one hurt his little girl.

He turned at the scratch at the door. "Yes."

Lady Crampton entered the room. He always

smiled when he saw her. The best thing he'd done in ages was hire her to chaperone the girls. After the trouble Elise got into last year, he was sure everything was aboveboard where Juliet was concerned. Lady Crampton did a superb job of keeping an eye on things. No more early babies.

Despite his anger, he gave her a warm smile. She had certainly brought a lot of happiness to the house since her arrival. "Yes, Selina, what is it?" Sometime back they had reverted to first names when in private.

"Maxwell, I need for you to sit down. I have something to tell you."

"Certainly. You look quite serious." He waved her to a seat by the fireplace, a little concerned that she was intending to leave him. He could never allow that. Marigold would need her next year.

The devil take it. His thoughts began to churn. Had she found a man at one of these events that wanted to marry her? Of course, that was a possibility. She was certainly an attractive woman. He had no idea why, but that unsettled him more than he wished. Pushing that thought to the back of his mind, he said, "You seem a bit troubled. What is the problem?"

"Now, Maxwell, I want you to remain calm while I tell you this."

He moved forward in his seat, his heart pounding. "The devil take it, Selina. You cannot leave! Marigold will have her Season next year, and I need you to see to it."

Her eyes grew wide at his tone. "I have no intention of leaving."

He broke into a smile. "Good. Good. Now what is it you wanted to see me about?"

Eyeing him strangely, she said, "I met with Lord Hertford a short time ago."

"What! Is the bounder back in town? I shall invite him to Gentleman Jim's and have a go at him. I am not too old to beat that blackguard. He will pay for the distress he has caused my daughter."

She shook her head. "Now, Maxwell, I specifically asked you to remain calm." She waved her hand at him. "This is hardly calm."

"I do not understand you, the mother of two little girls. Would you not wreak havoc on a man who treated one of your daughters in such a cavalier way?"

"Certainly, and you must know I feel the same for Marigold and Juliet as I do for my own little girls. However, I have reason to believe there is more to the story than what meets the eye."

Pomeroy jumped up and strode to the sideboard. "Would you care for a sherry?"

"Yes. I believe I would."

He poured himself a brandy, and brought a glass of sherry to Selina. She took a sip and closed her eyes. He stared at her as her throat worked, and felt a flush of heat he hadn't felt in quite a long time.

She opened her eyes and he quickly closed the mouth he hadn't realized hung open. "When I confronted Lord Hertford with the story Lady Windham told me, he was extremely upset, but not for the obvious reason. He seemed much more frustrated than embarrassed or guilty. He told me there is much more to the story, but unfortunately, he was unable to elaborate because of a promise he'd made."

Pomeroy snorted. "So, he cannot say what the rest of the tale is, but expects us to forgive and forget? Not bloody likely."

"Maxwell! Language."

He grinned at her sheepishly. "I apologize, 'twas not well done of me, I'm afraid."

She nodded an acceptance of his apology. "In any event, he asked that we escort Juliet to an estate in Suffolk that belonged to the late Duke of Reading. He assures me there is someone in residence there who can explain it all to her."

Pomeroy shook his head. "She will never consent." He studied Selina for a minute. "Tell me, and I trust your judgment. Do you feel whoever this person is he wants us to see, and the story he will tell, might change things? Just might ease Juliet's suffering?"

"It is truly hard for me to say. But my instincts tell me that Lord Hertford is very much in love with Juliet, and is convinced once she hears what this person in Suffolk has to say, she will change her mind."

Pomeroy rubbed his chin. "I do want her to be happy, and she certainly is not happy right now."

Selina remained silent, just watching him.

"Very well. We will kidnap Juliet. First thing in the morning. Send word to Hertford to send our driver the direction, and then meet us there tomorrow." He sat back and sipped his brandy. "This better be good. Perhaps I should bring my pistol with me."

"My lord!"

CHAPTER TWELVE

Juliet covered her mouth with her hand to stifle a yawn as she climbed into the carriage behind Lady Crampton. Papa settled in next. "Papa, I don't understand this hurried-up trip to our country estate. I hardly had time for Charlene to pack enough clothes for a week. And why isn't Marigold going with us? This is all so confusing."

Lady Crampton patted Juliet's hand. "Marigold has so many events she is schedule to attend, it would be unkind to drag her away."

"Then who will chaperone her?"

"Not to worry, my dear. Lady Albright has volunteered to help out."

Lady Crampton had barged her way into her room last night and told her it was time for her to get out of the house. It seemed she and Papa had planned a trip to Pomeroy Manor for Papa to see to some problem with the estate, and they thought it was a good time for her to take a short trip away from London. Why Lady Crampton was going with them remained a mystery because when she questioned her, she gave some convoluted explanation, and then waved her hand toward her wardrobe and suggested she chose what she wanted to bring with her.

She was certainly happy to get way from London, with all the memories she was trying desperately to forget. And truth be known, she was quite tired of sitting in her room and staring at herself in the mirror. She had even drunk the chocolate Charlene prepared for her earlier, and ate two warm rolls with butter.

She had realized yesterday if she was, in fact, carrying Graham's child—curse him—she needed to eat. If she could focus on that, and sweep everything aside, she could get through one day at a time. When the time came, she would retire to Elise's home in the country, have the babe, and then return to her family's estate with her child, never again to return to London to face the scandal.

"Why don't you lie back and get some more rest?" Lady Crampton pulled out a blanket and small pillow from under her seat and handed it to her.

"Very well. I am feeling a bit under the weather." She fell asleep to comforting sound of the carriage wheels and the low murmuring of Lady Crampton and Papa. It almost reminded her of when she was quite young and the family would take trips. Mama always tucked her and her sisters in, and they slept a good part of the trip to the comfort of their parents' voices.

"Wake up sleepyhead." Papa's deep voice stirred her from her slumber. She sat up and stretched. "We're not there already?"

"No. We've stopped to change horses and have something to eat. "

"Good." She threw the blanket off and sat up. "I'm quite hungry." She didn't miss the smirk Papa offered to Lady Crampton. She, on the other hand studied Juliet with narrowed eyes. Certainly, the woman did not guess that Juliet suspected she was increasing?

Once Papa helped her out, she looked around. "I don't remember ever passing this inn before."

Papa's eyes grew wide and he coughed. "We are taking a different road this time. The driver tells me he hears the one we usually travel is in bad shape." He put his arm around her shoulder and moved her forward, chatting about bad roads, stuck carriage wheels, horses going lame, and a number of other things she did not understand.

The afternoon ride was pleasant, and Juliet's black mood had begun to life. Not that she was not still angry and depressed. It seemed the more miles between her and London, the more she relaxed. She would enjoy this trip, and put everything else at the back of her mind, to be dealt with later.

It had grown too dim to continue reading her book. She closed it just as the carriage came to a rolling stop. "Are we at the inn?"

"Er, no." Papa looked toward Lady Crampton. She fidgeted with her skirts, not looking at either Papa or her. Juliet glanced between the two of them. Something odd was going on. She gathered her reticule, and the bonnet she had removed earlier just as the door to the carriage opened. "Good evening, my lord, ladies."

All the blood left her face, and her eyes grew wide. Graham had opened the door and stood not three feet from her. "Hello, Juliet."

She reared back on the seat, her eyes flicking between Papa and Lady Crampton. "How dare you! Why have you brought me to this . . . this . . . this person!"

Papa looked as though he wanted to make a dash for it, but Lady Crampton held her ground. She extended her hand to Juliet. "My dear, Lord Hertford wishes you to meet someone, and hear a story he has not been permitted to reveal." She tilted her head. "Please?"

Another pack of lies? Another way to make a fool of her? Certainly, not. She burrowed herself into the corner of the carriage. "No."

Graham ran his fingers through his hair. "Please, Juliet. Just give me a half hour. That's all I ask."

She narrowed her eyes at him. "What sort of lies have you told to Lady Crampton and Papa to have them trick me into coming here?"

"He told me no lies because he hasn't told me anything," Lady Crampton said. "However, he has convinced me if we all came here, the issue that has been standing between you two will be resolved."

Juliet snorted. Most unladylike. "And you believe him? I, on the other hand, can't believe he could fool you as he fooled me."

"If his story does not correct the situation, not only will we all return home post haste, but I will see that the man is ruined." Papa narrowed his eyes at Graham. "Is that clear, young man?"

"Yes, sir." He did not look the least concerned about Papa's threat. That did give her pause. Papa held a lot of sway in the *ton*, and if Graham ever expected to have a social life among Polite Society, it was best not to cross the Earl of Pomeroy. He reached his hand out. "Juliet?"

***

Graham breathed a sigh of relief when Juliet moved forward and took his hand. He was still stunned that Lady Crampton had approached him two days ago. She seemed eager to have him redeem himself, and he was relieved when she agreed to his plan. He had no idea how they got Juliet all the way out here, but based on her reaction when she saw him, they had not told her the truth.

She refused to accept his arm, but took her father's arm instead, with Lady Crampton on the other side of Pomeroy. They all entered the duke's country estate where Amy and Boyle awaited them.

It had taken some effort on his part to convince Mr. Boyle to agree to this plan. Very protective of Amy, at first he refused, insisting her name would be damaged among the "coxcombs and dandies" in London, which was what her father had attempted to prevent.

When Amy pleaded her case on Grahams' behalf, assuring Boyle that she had no intention of ever being among the *ton* again, since her life was with him, he relented. It appeared to Graham's eyes that there was very little the man could deny Amy. In fact, Graham had planned to tell them as soon as this mess with Juliet was cleared up that they had his permission to marry.

Graham led Lady Crampton, Lord Pomeroy, and Juliet into the drawing room. Boyle stood as they all entered and bowed to the two ladies. Graham took Juliet's elbow and escorted her to a chair across from Amy. Juliet's chin rose, and Graham had the feeling she knew who Amy was, just not her relationship to Graham. He had to get the words out quickly before she bolted again.

"Lady Amy, I would like to present to you, Lady Juliet Smith, Lady Crampton, her companion, and Lord Pomeroy, Lady Juliet's father." He turned to the three of them. "May I present Lady Amy Andrews, daughter of the late Duke of Reading."

Juliet's eyes widened, and he knew he had her

attention.

"Lady Amy has a story to tell all of you. It is a tale that began with the duke last summer, but since I promised him I would never discuss it, I have been unable to defend myself against unjust charges."

Amy reached for Boyle's hand and he gave her a warm smile. "My lord, my ladies, I am pleased to meet you. For a number of reasons. Graham has been like a brother to me since we grew up together in this very house when my papa became his guardian. I love him, and it would break my heart if something he had nothing to do with, and was merely protecting me, and helping Papa, made him lose his own happiness."

She stood and walked over to Juliet and sat alongside her, taking her hands in hers. "He loves you very much, my lady. And I know that because he told me so, and Graham never lies."

Juliet glanced at him, and chewed her lip. She then turned her attention back to Amy, and Amy proceeded to tell her tale in a very adult manner, which pleased, and surprised, Graham. Several times she would glance at Boyle, as if needing his strength, and then take a deep breath and continue. Once she finished speaking, she, Juliet, and Lady Crampton were all patting their eyes with their handkerchiefs.

The men were tugging on their neckcloths, and eyeing the door, looking for an escape.

Juliet drew herself up, and her eyes flashing, turned on Graham. "How dare you not allow these two to marry? And how dare you not leave this very minute to retrieve their child?" She stood and marched over to him. An angel of righteousness.

He backed up when she leaned over him. "Despite the late duke's desire to protect his daughter, he has done her a terrible injustice." She poked him in the chest. "If you are the man I thought you were, there will be a wedding this afternoon, and then you will purchase tickets for the next packet out of Dover so Mr. and Mrs. Boyle can go to Paris and get their baby back."

The room was stunned into silence. After a few moments, Lady Crampton stood and shook out her skirts. "I suggest we all retire to another room" —she turned to Amy— "can we use your papa's library?"

Amy swung her gaze to Lady Crampton. "Yes, we can use the library."

"Good. I believe Lord Hertford and Lady Juliet need some time together, and it appears we have two weddings to plan." What that statement, she turned to Pomeroy with raised eyebrows. He scrambled to his feet and followed her out as she marched to the door like a military commander, with Amy and Boyle falling in behind her. The door closed quietly and he looked up at Juliet.

What did he see in her eyes? Obviously, the story Amy had told would have convinced her he'd done no wrong. But her tirade about him not allowing them to marry may have only put another bee in her bonnet.

Women were difficult to understand under the best of circumstances.

He opened his mouth to speak and she quickly put her finger to his lips. "No. Don't say anything yet. I am still trying to accept all that I've just heard." She leaned back and smiled at him. "You must admit, it did not look good for you."

Encouraged by her soft tone and slight smile, he tugged her hand until she fell on his lap. He wrapped his arms around her waist. "I wanted more than anything to tell you the entire story when I returned this year. But my promise to the duke was sacred, and then before I could ask his permission to at least tell you to clear myself in your eyes, he had a stroke and could not speak."

"It was quite honorable of you to keep your promise when it would have been so easy to break it and save yourself a lot of anguish."

He shook his head. "It never occurred to me to do that. One thing the late duke taught me was honor. A gentleman's word is his honor. Without that, I have nothing."

Juliet twirled one of the curls that had escaped her topknot and smiled. "The banns have already been called."

"Yes."

"Everyone who means the most to us is here, except Marigold and Lady Crampton's daughters.

We could send for them."

"Yes?" Where was she going with this? Hopefully right where he wanted her to go.

He raised his brows. "And?"

"And we could have a double wedding if Mr. Boyle could get a special license."

"No."

Juliet's face fell. "No?"

"No. He would not be able to obtain a special license. But, as Amy's guardian, I could petition for one for them." He broke into a grin that soon had Juliet grinning at him. Right before he took her mouth in a searing kiss.

***

Two brides and two grooms stood before the vicar in the very same chapel the late Duke of Reading had been buried from a few weeks earlier.

After a flurry of activity orchestrated by Lady Crampton, the weddings were ready to proceed. Cook had come through with a wonderful wedding breakfast that awaited the family and few friends who attended the weddings of Lady Amy Andrews, daughter of the late Duke of Reading, to Mr. Francis Boyle, bookseller and farmer, and Lady Juliet Smith, daughter of the Earl of Pomeroy to the Honorable, the Marquess of Hertford.

Lady Marigold, Lady Prudence, and Lady Phoebe had been summoned from London, and Lord and Lady St George from their country estate. There had been a great deal of oohing and aahing over the baby St. George.

Juliet had spent the last few days getting to know Lady Amy, and found her delightful, charming and very funny. Whatever deficiencies she suffered from made no difference to anyone who knew and loved her. And Mr. Francis Boyle saw no shortcomings whatsoever. More than once he stated all he wanted to do for the rest of his life was take care of Amy and their children.

Graham had dispatched a note to the foundling home in Paris, advising them that the baby Lady Agneaux had placed with them last year would soon be retrieved by the child's parents. No one knew, just yet, if the baby had been a girl or a boy. The parents were excited to discover if they had a son or a daughter. Mr. Boyle had advised them all that he would be happy with either, and planned to have many more.

The last wishes for the happiness of the couples had been offered, and the final bottle of champagne emptied when Graham and Juliet ascended the stairs to the bedchamber they were to occupy for the night. The next day, while the Boyles were headed to Paris, she and Graham would travel to his estate for a few weeks, forgoing the rest of the Season.

Juliet mused that some tales did have happy endings, as Graham closed the door to the bedchamber, turned and moved toward her with a stealth that had her shivering.

She liked shivers.

***

"Two beautiful weddings, were they not?" Lord Pomeroy sat next to Lady Crampton on the settee in the late duke's drawing room, a half empty glass of champagne in each of their hands. She had kicked off her slippers and tucked her feet underneath her.

"Truly. I am so very happy it all worked out for both couples. They are wonderful young people, and deserve happiness." She smiled as she stared into the fireplace, a pensive look on her face.

"And you? Do you deserve happiness?" Bloody hell, why did he ask that question? With just the two of them sitting here, things appeared much too cozy for his peace of mind. He'd had his happiness with Florence, all those years ago. Now he looked forward to his daughters all marrying and presenting him with grandchildren to play with, and send home.

"I am happy," she said softly.

After several minutes had passed and she hadn't elaborated, he cleared his throat in an attempt to break whatever ridiculous spell had been cast upon him. "Two daughters happily married and one more to go."

Selina looked over at him. "Yes. I believe Marigold will be ready next year to accept suitors. She's a lovely girl, and received some attention already this Season."

"You did a splendid job chaperoning Juliet." He patted her hand.

She smiled, and he swore she said, "Not quite, my lord."

They both turned at the sound of Hertford's shout. "I'm to be a father?!"

The End

Did you like this story? Please consider leaving a review on either Goodreads or the place where you bought it. Long or short, your review will help other readers discover new authors and make purchasing decisions!

Want to read more Regency romance from Callie Hutton? Turn the page for an excerpt from *For the Love of the Viscount,* Book 1 in the Noble Hearts series.

FOR THE LOVE OF THE VISCOUNT

Prologue

London, England
March, 1818

The Right Honorable, the Earl of Pomeroy, sat at the head of his dinner table and smiled at his three lovely daughters, who smiled back at him. Three *unmarried* lovely daughters. Each one was charming and pretty in her own way. And each one needed to find a husband and remove herself from his benevolence before he went broke.

The bills continued to pile up on the desk in his study. Bonnets, gowns, gloves, slippers, ribbons. The list was endless. While he had no doubt his two youngest daughters, Lady Juliet and Lady Marigold, would one day find their way to the altar, he had no expectations that his eldest, Lady Elise at three and twenty, would ever wander in that direction. Without a little push, that was.

Which he was about to give.

"My dears, I would like your attention, if you please." He smiled at the loves of his life. Obedient as ever, they all gave him their utmost attention. One pair of blue eyes, two hazel.

"Yes, Papa?" Elise, one of the pair of hazel eyes, said.

He cleared this throat. "It has come to my attention that perhaps I have been remiss in assuring all of you secure the best in life. Everything that your blessed mother—" he made the sign of the cross "—and I, had together. Love, marriage, children."

Julie and Marigold continued to smile, but Elise stiffened and a frown marred her comely face. *Ah, yes.* That was expected.

"Of course we wish that for ourselves as well," his youngest darling, Lady Marigold, said. A true treasure, and the image of her exquisite mother.

"Indeed."

"Papa, I believe we spoke of this before." Elise patted her mouth with her serviette and laid it alongside her plate. "Marigold and Juliet are well suited to marriage, but I thought we agreed I would continue on here with you. You know I do an excellent job of managing your house."

"And my life as well, my dear." He gave her a well-rehearsed fatherly smile.

"What did you have in mind, Papa? The Season is just starting, and I hope to find my true love this year." Juliet, at nine and ten years, brought sunshine and happiness to his life. Along with a pile of bills for jewelry and shoes. Lord, the girl loved shoes and dance slippers. She must dance every dance at every ball since she went through two pairs at each event.

"I believe the best way to assure each of you has what every woman dreams of is a sensible method I have spent many a night deciding on."

Two of his daughters stared at him with excitement since it sounded as though this was a plan to help them obtain their wishes and hopes. Alas, Elise apparently found the conversation disturbing. She did not look in his eyes when he gazed at her. He was aware his normal look of adoration had a bit of determination in it.

"What have you decided, Papa? Since I have no interest in marriage—*as you well know*—this plan is most likely for my sisters. I want to be sure it will be the best idea for them." She wagged her finger at him. "You do come up with a scheme that is less than ideal on occasion, in which case I have needed to direct you toward another avenue."

Yes the love of my heart, you spend a great deal of time directing.

The moment had arrived. "It seems fair to me that you should all find your husbands in order." He sat back and beamed as if he'd discovered the secret of longevity.

His beloved Elise frowned. "In order of what?"

"Birth."

Elise continued to stare at him, her mouth agape. Juliet asked, "Birth?"

"Yes, my dear hearts. We will spend the next weeks seeing that our darling Elise finds her perfect match, as she is the firstborn of my delightful progeny."

Juliet and Marigold gasped in horror and looked at their sister. Elise had made it known quite loudly, and often, that she had no intention of marrying.

Ever.

Elise cleared her through. "Papa, I assume you are joking with us."

He turned his attention to her, forcing his steely determination to overwhelm the adoration. "No, my precious. It came to me in a dream where I saw your beloved mother who took me to task for allowing you to flounder when I should be guiding you."

"Flounder? Guiding?" His poor girl's face was pale, her breathing rapid.

She seemed to steady herself and put forth her brightest smile. "Oh, Papa. While I appreciate your concern for my future, I believe we can turn our efforts and attention to Juliet." Her lips tightened, and she glared at her sister, apparently looking for support.

"I agree, Papa. I would love to have help from all of you in securing my future." His sweet second eldest nudged Marigold with her elbow.

"Ouch. Yes, Papa, I think Juliet is definitely the one we should be focused on. My turn will be next year." Marigold rubbed her side and cast a reproving glance at her sister.

"Oh, my enchanting offspring, how I love you so. However, my mind is made up. We will see Elise a happy bride this year." He beamed at them, looking from one cherished daughter to the next. 'Twas time for others—with hefty bank rolls—to cherish them as well.

"Papa, suppose I refuse?" Elise had never gone against his wishes in her entire life. She had always been able to persuade him to see things her way. Which was another advantage to his plan. She would be directing someone else's life.

"Then, my dear, I am afraid it will take longer for your sisters to find their own true loves. You see, I will be unable to accept suitors for them until you are safely settled in your own little love nest." With that pronouncement he stood and gave them a slight bow. "Now if you will excuse me, I will retire to my library and enjoy a brandy before bed."

Three girls sat opened-mouth as he smiled at them and left the room. He strode down the corridor, lighthearted. He'd put his plan into action, and soon he would be free of bills. Not that he begrudged his treasured daughters their fribbles, but a man could not watch his fortune dwindle every day without concern.

Although he had no son to whom he would pass along his title and money, it still disturbed him to watch his balance shrink monthly.

Grinning to himself, he poured a brandy and sat by the fireplace, raising a toast to freedom.

Now Available!
Visit your favorite online retailer to keep reading
For the Love of the Viscount.

ABOUT THE AUTHOR

Callie Hutton, the *USA Today* bestselling author of *The Elusive Wife,* writes both Western Historical and Regency romance, with "historic elements and sensory details" (*The Romance Reviews*). She also pens an occasional contemporary or two. Callie lives in Oklahoma with several rescue dogs and her top cheerleader husband of many years. Her family also includes her daughter, son, daughter-in-law and twin grandsons affectionately known as "The Twinadoes."

Callie loves to hear from readers. Contact her directly at calliehutton11@gmail.com or find her online at www.calliehutton.com. Sign up for her newsletter to receive information on new releases, appearances, contests and exclusive subscriber content. Visit her on Facebook, Twitter and Goodreads.

Callie Hutton has written more than 25 books. For a complete listing, go to www.calliehutton.com/books

Praise for books by Callie Hutton

A Wife by Christmas

"A *Wife by Christmas* is the reason why we read romance...the perfect story for any season." --The Romance Reviews Top Pick

The Elusive Wife

"I loved this book and you will too. Jason is a hottie

& Oliva is the kind of woman we'd all want as a friend. Read it!" --Cocktails and Books

"In my experience I've had a few hits but more misses with historical romance so I was really pleasantly surprised to be hooked from the start by obviously good writing." --Book Chick City

"The historic elements and sensory details of each scene make the story come to life, and certainly helps immerse the reader in the world that Olivia and Jason share." --The Romance Reviews

"You will not want to miss *The Elusive Wife*." --My Book Addiction

"...it was a well written plot and the characters were likeable." --Night Owl Reviews

A Run for Love

"An exciting, heart-warming Western love story!" --*NY Times* bestselling author Georgina Gentry

"I loved this book!!! I read the BEST historical romance last night...It's called *A Run For Love*.: --*NY Times* bestselling author Sharon Sala

"This is my first Callie Hutton story, but it certainly won't be my last." --The Romance Reviews

A Prescription for Love

"There was love, romance, angst, some darkness,

laughter, hope and despair." --RomCon

"I laughed out loud at some of the dialogue and situations. I think you will enjoy this story by Callie Hutton." --Night Owl Reviews

An Angel in the Mail

"…a warm fuzzy sensuous read. I didn't put it down until I was done." --Sizzling Hot Reviews

Visit www.calliehutton.com for more information.

55499658R00109

Made in the USA
Columbia, SC
14 April 2019